Jean de la Fontaine was born in 1... Château Thierry, the son of a provincial official. A scholar and a poet he was deeply read in the classics, both ancient and modern. He was brought up in the countryside, where later as Maître des Eaux et Forêts he inherited, but eventually sold, his father's post. He spent most of his adult years in Paris and was for a short time attached to the Oratoire, and for much longer in touch with Port Royal. He appears to have obtained a licence to practise as a lawyer, but there is no record of him having done so. He was maintained by a series of patrons including the chancellor Foucquet, to whom he remained loyal after his fall in 1661, the Duke of Bouillon and the cultured and brilliant Mme de la Sablière. His fame rests on his *Fables* for which he drew on the great Aesopian treasury, which had been constantly exploited by French writers since the Middle Ages, and on the Indian fables of Bidpai. His originality was to revive the fable in verse, little practised since the sixteenth century. His other main work is his verse *Contes*, whose licentious themes are often borrowed from Boccaccio, Ariosto or Rabelais. He wrote other miscellaneous poems and re-told in prose the classical myth of Psyche, and also wrote the libretti of three operas. He died in Paris in 1695.

James Michie was born in 1927 and educated at Marlborough and Trinity College, Oxford, where he read Classics. He is at present a director of The Bodley Head. His publications include a book of poems, *Possible Laughter*, and Latin translations *Horace : The Odes*, *Catullus : The Poems* and *Martial : The Epigrams*.

La Fontaine: Selected Fables

TRANSLATED BY JAMES MICHIE

INTRODUCTION BY GEOFFREY GRIGSON

PENGUIN BOOKS

Penguin Books Ltd, Harmondsworth, Middlesex, England
Penguin Books, 625 Madison Avenue, New York, New York 10022, U.S.A.
Penguin Books Australia Ltd, Ringwood, Victoria, Australia
Penguin Books Canada Ltd, 2801 John Street, Markham, Ontario, Canada L3R 1B4
Penguin Books (N.Z.) Ltd, 182-190 Wairau Road, Auckland 10, New Zealand

First published by Allen Lane 1979
This edition published in Penguin Books 1982

The title-page illustration is from the edition published by
H. Fournier Aîné, Paris, 1842.

Made and printed in Great Britain by
Cox & Wyman Ltd, Reading

TO GILLON AITKEN

CONTENTS

JEAN DE LA FONTAINE

1621–95

An endearing but far from irrelevant sketch of La Fontaine when he was young has come down to us in the *Historiettes* of his friend Gidéon Tallemant des Réaux, a banker's son, who was the John Aubrey of seventeenth-century France.

The year would have been about 1648 or 1649, when La Fontaine was in his late twenties. He had made friends with Tallemant, among other young writers and young poets, when he was a law student in Paris. But he was unknown, and it was not his still un-exhibited genius which Tallemant celebrated. It was his remarkable absence of mind. Tallemant brought him into the *Historiettes*, unfledged, to round off an account of one or two eccentric dreamers, first of whom was the country-courtier poet Racan of established name and of a much earlier generation.

'Among these very absent-minded people,' wrote Tallemant (who was three years older than La Fontaine), 'is a young man of letters who also writes verse, called La Fontaine. His father, the super-intendent of waters and forests of Château-Thierry in Champagne, was in Paris once for a lawsuit and said to him, "Go and do such and such for me straightaway, it's urgent." La Fontaine went off and was no sooner out of the house than he forgot what his father had said to him. He ran into some friends, who asked if he was doing anything. "No," he replied, and away they all went to the playhouse. Another time, when he was going to Paris, he tied a large bag of important papers to his saddle-bow. He did not do it properly and the bag fell off. The post-boy came by, picked up the bag, found La Fontaine and asked him if he had lost anything. The young man looked about him. "No," he said, "I have not lost anything," "I have found this bag," said the post-boy – "But that's my bag!" cried La Fontaine. "Everything I have is in that bag." And he carried it all the way home in his arms.

Once, when there was a hard frost, this young man walked a full ten miles from Château-Thierry, at night, in his kid boots, carrying a lantern in his hand with the light shuttered off.

Another time he kidnapped the little dog – it was a very good watch-dog – from the house where the lady of the lieutenant-governor of Château-Thierry lived. Then when the husband was away he hid himself in her bedroom below a table covered with a cloth. The lady had one of her women-friends sleeping in with her. As soon as he noticed that this friend was snoring he went over to the bed, took hold of the hand of the lieutenant-governor's wife, who was still awake but fortunately did not scream, and at the same time whispered his name. She took this as such a mark of love that I believe – though La Fontaine said he was allowed only the giblets – only to goose her up – that the lady granted him everything. He left before the friend was awake; and as in such little towns people are always in and out of each other's houses nobody thought it odd to see him coming at such an early hour out of a house which was more or less open.

Later on his father found him a wife, whom he married to be obliging. His wife says he is so absent-minded that sometimes he will let three weeks go by without remembering he is a husband. Her own behaviour with men has been irregular enough for some time, but it does not worry him. He was told "So and so has been after your wife." "I'faith," he replied, "he can do as he likes. I don't care. He will be just as bored as I have been." This indifference infuriates her. She is eaten up with vexation, and he finds love where he can. He lodged an "abbess" who had taken herself to Château-Thierry, and one day his wife surprised them. He left off, and walked away.'

There is no need to doubt Tallemant des Réaux's anecdotes. They fit, and he knew his friend. And the lieutenant-governor's lady was surely, like most people in La Fontaine's life, quite unable to disregard his naïvety and charm; which like other of his personal qualities related in fact to the qualities of his verse.

As we shall see, heritage and circumstances conspired for him, all contributing to the writings of a poet whose celebrated absence of mind, on the *ex post facto* view, really indicated the acutest presence of mind elsewhere, its most thorough cultivation in other directions; a poet, certainly, who liked to please and be pleased, and yet one who found that worst of literary sins, ingratiation in the substance of his verse, as unnecessary as it would have been repugnant.

La Fontaine, in these considerations, required only to be La Fontaine, as in the end he realized.

Little is known about Jean de la Fontaine's early life at Château-Thierry, though much can be inferred, above all from its evident contribution to the *Fables*, in years ahead.

Château-Thierry is a small castle town on the Marne, penetrated then, as it continues to be, by country concerns. Yet it was only fifty miles or so east of Paris, a market town linked to sophistication by what was at the time the great highway from Paris into the heart of Europe, the road which wriggled through the valley of the Marne, and continued via Châlons and Nancy to Strasbourg, and on across the Rhine up to Frankfurt.

If Paris was so close, if metropolitan influences came inevitably down the road, round about Château-Thierry there extended a microcosm of familiar woods, waters and meadows. La Fontaine had the freedom of this neighbourhood, this native ground. 'Brook' and 'meadow', *ruisseau* and *pré*, are two of his favourite words –

> Ils arrivèrent dans un pré
> Tout bordé de ruisseaux, de fleurs tout diapré
> où maint mouton cherchait la vie.

Moreover at Château-Thierry – one cannot think of La Fontaine growing up in a sour country of clay and cider or clay and beer – the Champagne vineyards begin.

In this heavily green countryside which was neither a hell nor a paradise nor an Ultima Thule, La Fontaine's family lived above poverty and mediocrity (though not above debt eventually), and below wealth. His father's royal posts as Maître des Eaux et Forêts and Captain of the Chase should have made the characters and peculiarities of the peasants, of the woodcutters, huntsmen, fisher-men, carters and the like, extra familiar to his son, who had an ear for pâtois, and could no doubt see the townspeople, the coopers, carpenters, cobblers, butchers, barrel makers, the corn-merchants, the shop-keepers, notaries, etc., with country acuity, and the country people equally with the townsman's eye.

La Fontaine senior respected learning and literature; and La Fontaine, whether at home in Château-Thierry or up the road in Paris, or both, was unquestionably well educated; as well as highly intelli-gent and responsive.

He was the elder of two sons. Absent-minded or no, he would succeed his father in his official posts, in the ordinary course. But in 1641, when he was twenty, there seems to have been thought of turning him into a priest. In Paris he was enrolled with the Orator-ians, the great educators for the priesthood in this era of the Counter-Reformation. That improbable interlude in La Fontaine's life lasted – not surprisingly – no more than eighteen months or so, as if the call of such as the lieutenant-governor's lady was too fre-quent and too enticing; and La Fontaine came back again to Château-Thierry.

Law would be more useful than theology in his official dealings in the future with woodcutters, water-men and hunters, so a student of law he became in his mid-twenties, and then a full-feathered advocate, in that other Parisian sector of his life when he grew into intimacy with Tallemant, with François Maucroix, Paul Pellisson, and other young writers of his own age who were to become distinguished in literature or as officials, or eventually, some of them, as members of the new *Académie française* (like La Fontaine himself at last).

This early grouping of La Fontaine with friends is a good example of Sainte-Beuve's principle of examining the first milieu, the first keepings, of a writer among writers – 'the natural and as it were spontaneous association of young minds and young talents – not exactly alike or of the same family, but of the same flight and the same springtime, hatched under the same planet, and feeling themselves born – despite differences in taste and calling – to work to a common end, to flower under the same sun.' Indeed Sainte-Beuve was thinking of La Fontaine, though of La Fontaine some years on, in his forties, in a grander group consisting of Boileau, Racine, and Molière, all geniuses together, as Sainte-Beuve exclaimed.

What is certain in the uncertainties about La Fontaine in his twenties and then in his thirties, besides his marriage (1647) and its failure, an involvement in legal and other work of the Waters and Forests at Château-Thierry, the publication of his first book, a version of Terence's comedy the *Eunuchus* (1654), the death of his father (1658) and his succession to his father's local offices, is that if his mind absented itself much from prudential affairs, it became more and more fixed now on writing and learning. Was it verses he had in his head, or a woman, or both, on that long frosty walk which Tallemant recorded, wearing the wrong boots and clutching the lantern which was giving no light.

As usual the absent mind was present elsewhere.

That other presence, that integrity, we can read in a portrait of La Fontaine by François de Troy, painted in the later years of his celebrity as the poet of the *Fables* and the *Contes et Nouvelles*. It shows a face sensual, humorous, still unlined, in a way both concerned and unconcerned, with a wide generous mouth; and with eyes, in control of the face, yet detached from the incidental, which measure the spectator, and look beyond him as well. It seems to me a face not quite easy to endure: this daft man may be seeing deeper into us than we suppose. But it put no one off.

La Fontaine's thirty-seventh, thirty-eighth year, 1658, seems crucial. His father dies, he and his wife divide their property and continue a life at Château-Thierry of united separation, in the family house alongside the ruins of the castle. But he had finished, for some while, and he now offers to the grandest, richest, most cultured if also most swaggering of patrons, young Louis XIV's finance minister Foucquet, a first long poem, 'ces fruits de ma solitude'.

This was La Fontaine's *Adonis*. It came to Foucquet, that strange, extravagant mixture of a man, when he was recovering from a severe illness, so no doubt he found time to read it to the end, before returning to manipulate the revenues and planning his great château and gardens some sixty miles away to the south-west at Vaux-le-Vicomte (a work on which 18,000 workmen were employed). Foucquet would surely have recognized in the opening lines a new melodic voice of freedom and lightness and charm:

> Je n'ai pas entrepris de chanter dans ces vers
> Rome ni ses enfants vainqueurs de l'Univers,
> Ni les fameuses tours qu'Hector ne put défendre,
> Ni les combats des dieux aux rives du Scamandre.
> Ces sujets sont trop hauts, et je manque de voix:
> Je n'ai jamais chanté que l'ombrage des bois,
> Flore, Écho, les Zephyrs, et leurs molles haleines,
> Le vert tapis des prés et l'argent des fontaines.
> C'est parmi les forêts qu'a vécu mon héros;
> C'est dans les bois qu'Amour a troublé son repos

– a voice which could speak of the long darkness which is the end of grace and gaiety, as when Venus, goddess as she may be, mourns Adonis and exclaims in despair

> Je demande un moment, et ne puis l'obtenir.
> Noires divinités du ténébreux empire,
> Dont le pouvoir s'étend sur tout ce qui respire,
> Rois des peuples légers, souffrez que mon amant
> De son triste départ me console un moment.

Vous ne le perdrez point: le trésor que je pleure
Ornera tôt ou tard votre sombre demeure.
Quoi! vous me refusez un présent si léger?

Foucquet no doubt took La Fontaine on trust at first from his able
secretary, that Paul Pellisson, writer and poet, who had been one of
young La Fontaine's intimates in Paris, at the time of his law
studies. He granted La Fontaine a pension, enlisting him among the
prize adjuncts of Vaux-le-Vicomte – Le Vau for the château, Le
Brun for its decoration, Le Nôtre for its garden embroidery, Vatel
for its banquets, and now, if he could live up to his *Adonis*, La Fon-
taine for its poetry. La Fontaine's first duty was to write, in praise
of the grand château and its gardens, a poem which he proposed to
call *Le Songe de Vaux*, the Dream of Vaux, the dream, dramatic,
lyrical, allegorical, mythological, rather than descriptive, of what the
Vaux gardens, newly planted and only shrub-high, would be in years
to come.

It was a poem La Fontaine never finished (though later on a few
fragments were published, some in La Fontaine's lifetime) because
in 1661, after he had been three years his pensioner, Foucquet
was arrested and disgraced, on the way to imprisonment for
life.

In that famous and too gorgeous fête, in August 1661, which
inaugurated the château and its gardens and so angered the twenty-
three-year-old Louis XIV by its ostentation, triggering Foucquet's
arrest, La Fontaine's share had been to help in the first performance
of *Les Fâcheux*, Molière's *comédie-ballet* about the various bores who
interrupt the business of love, for which Pellisson, Foucquet's
secretary and La Fontaine's friend, had written the prologue.

Ill at first after his patron's dismissal and arrest, La Fontaine
recovered, and paid something of his debt to Foucquet, who was
being moved about from prison to prison, or château to château,
awaiting trial. He wrote and published, without his name to it, the
Élégie aux Nymphes de Vaux, reminding the nymphs that it was
Foucquet who had accommodated them so charmingly, and asking

them to soften the King towards Foucquet in his now terrible distress:

> Pour lui les plus beaux jours sont des secondes nuits:
> Les soucis dévorant, les regrets, les ennuis,
> Hôtes infortunés de sa triste demeure,
> En des gouffres de maux le plongent à toute heure.

He wrote a more direct 'Ode to the King', asking for clemency. In a letter from Amboise to his wife (their estrangement was not total or else had lessened for a while) he describes how Foucquet had been imprisoned there in the château, in a room – he had asked to see it – six feet across, without air except through a small high hole, every window blocked so that Foucquet could see nothing of the smiling extent of the Loire outside.

Caution was necessary, but though La Fontaine had lost his pension and his first patron, thanks to Foucquet (and Pellisson, whose share in the disaster was to spend six years in the Bastille) La Fontaine had been edging forward and mixing with his kind, at the level of his own genius. In 1664 he found another patron, a royal one, the dowager duchess of Orléans, and from then on until his death in 1695, La Fontaine was never without some grandee, man or especially woman, to lodge him or care for him.

When Foucquet crashed, La Fontaine was forty, on the confines of middle age, and he was still by no means a popular or widely known writer. He could see that more poems like *Adonis* or like *Le Songe de Vaux* could neither advance him in that way nor engage all of his poem-making strength and concern. So he took to stories of a different kind and weight – stories mostly about the escapades of love, and love-making, in both of which he was expert; and stories with a moral, implied or stated, stories or fables, wittily applicable to the quirks, frailties, follies and flourishes we are all aware of in others and overlook, as likely as not, in ourselves.

He was stepping towards greatness; but not in the *Contes et Nouvelles en vers*, which we shall consider first, dismissing them for the more astonishing originality, individuality and brio of the *Fables*.

La Fontaine wrote of his aim of pleasing and instructing in his poems – at least in his *Fables*. He might have said to any tight-lipped reader objecting to the *Contes* that, pleasing apart, he certainly instructed – in love, or taking advantage of girls. And his tongue, as he said so, would have been in and out of his cheek. When he was old, ill, in prospect of death, La Fontaine disavowed the *Contes*, but they are a part of him, all the same, part of the equilibrium of contradictions in himself, as they seem.

When he was young La Fontaine had made up a song about his dearest Maucroix, with whom he drank and womanized and idled and studied law. Maucroix gave up law for the priesthood and became a canon of Rheims. That was the occasion of this song of eight lines. One can imagine La Fontaine walking about, singing it:

> Tandis qu'il était avocat,
> Il n'a pas fait gain d'un ducat;
> Mais vive la canonicat!
>   Alleluia!
>
> Il lui rapporte force écus
> Qu'il veut au dieu Bacchus,
> Ou bien en faire des cocus!
>   Alleluia!

Improper. Impious. But then La Fontaine is the poet without a sense of guilt, or much sense of God, the poet of social man in the natural and unnatural world, the poet allying impropriety and propriety, gaiety and melancholy. Watch a butterfly in the sun, ranging flowers, and you find a new force in La Fontaine's celebrated description of himself as 'a butterfly on Parnassus', the mountain of Apollo and the Muses.

The first *Contes et Nouvelles en vers* came out four years after the dismissal of Foucquet, in 1665; a second batch appeared in 1666, a third in 1671; and the last, the *Nouveaux Contes* (the further sale of which was banned by order of the police, for locating too much of its indecency in nuns and priests), in 1675, when La Fontaine was fifty-four.

La Fontaine took his stories mostly from Boccaccio's *Decameron*, from the fifteenth-century *Les Cent Nouvelles Nouvelles*, and from Marguerite of Navarre's *Heptameron*. One or two of them came from Rabelais, one from Aretine. Remodelling them in his verse, he changed tale and incident as he pleased, and, as he declared (knowing that 'ce qui plaît en un temps peut ne pas plaire en un autre'), 'au goût de mon siècle'. But with a few fine exceptions they are tiresome, these up-dated and up-moded stories of cuckoldry, foolish girls, wily priests and the like. They can drop to a level of embarrassment and corniness of fun, as in the brief tale of the villager who lost his calf (No. XI in the second collection, taken from *Les Cent Nouvelles Nouvelles*). The villager goes and looks for his calf in the nearby forest. He climbs a tree which affords a listening post and a view out over the fields. Enter a lady, with a young gallant who sits down on the grass under the tree and exclaims about this lady standing by him ('en voyant je ne sais quel appas')

> 'O dieux! que vois-je! et que vois-je pas!'
> Sans dire quoi.

The villager up the tree interrupts:

> 'Homme de bien, qui voyez tant de choses.
> Voyez-vous point mon veau? dites-le moi.'

Which is all – and enough.

The versing of the *Contes* may be light, intimate, varied, often dramatic, but it reverberates too little. As for monotony of subject –

> Volontiers où soupçon séjourne
> Cocuage séjourne aussi

– it is fair to observe that in the last century the Belgian compiler of a French glossary explaining 'tous les mots consacrés à l'amour' was able to illustrate his words and phrases and euphemisms for our creating portions, male and female, and for our copulatory triumphs, with more than a hundred examples from La Fontaine's *Contes et Nouvelles* (he took an even greater number of examples from the works of La Fontaine's friend Tallemant).

A rum thing about the verse of La Fontaine's most active twenty years, from 1658, is its interleaving of the good and the tedious, of the *Fables* and the *Contes*; of *Adonis* (which was not published until 1669, and then without its dedication to Foucquet) and unexpected 'occasional' pieces which inclined to go on and on. But then La Fontaine became more and more a skilled versifier: friends or patrons asked, La Fontaine, self-critical or no, complied in his good nature: which explains the pietistic *Poème de la Captivité de Saint Malc*, of 1673, wedged, in its composition, among the later fables and the bawdier tales; or more oddly – though this was written much later, in his sixties – his poem in praise of quinine, new remedy for fevers.

To continue as a French or modern Ovid in elegant, and touching, verses, smoothly measured, or to go on writing *vers galants*, was insufficient for La Fontaine, convinced as he may have been (see the Preface to his *Amours de Psyché et de Cupidon*) that the taste of the era must always be considered, and that it was, in fact, attached firmly 'au galant et à la plaisanterie'. His course engaged too little of himself, and it was in the fable that this highly conscious, discerning, critical poet found the entire self-employment, the entire self-realization necessary to him.

In the spring of 1668, two years after the appearance of the second part of the *Contes et Nouvelles*, La Fontaine published the first six books of his *Fables choisies mises en vers*, a hundred and twenty-five of them, adding nearly a hundred more fables in the edition of 1678, and bringing out yet another two dozen in 1693, in his old age. A huge feat, seeing the level he kept.

'Mises en vers' – those are the words to mark in that first fabular title. Fables, of course, among the more ancient kinds of wisdom story, akin to wisdom in proverbs, were familiar to everyone – in prose. Aesop's fables were prose. The fables of Pilpay (Bidpai), from India, on which La Fontaine began to draw after that first fabulist offering of 1668, were prose. Prose – so far – had been the proper dress of fables. It is true that among the Ancients (whom La Fontaine so admired) one or two feeble writers, Phaedrus and Avienus in Latin, Babrius in Greek, had versified some of Aesop. It is true that Horace had slipped a fable or two into his satires and epistles. But then Phaedrus, Avienus, Babrius, and Horace, were not Frenchmen of the era of Versailles, and so far no Frenchman of genuine distinction as a poet had offered the public a book, a collection, of fables in verse.

Here then was La Fontaine, if a little slyly, using the familiar to launch his own poetry, here he was transforming the familiar and the instructive into poems of his own melody and structure; poems which would be replete with his grace – 'la grâce plus belle encore que la beauté' – his wit, his gaiety, his melancholy, his taste for the classics, or the classic myths, his amused experience of life, low, high and medium, in Château-Thierry, Paris, Vaux-le-Vicomte, his enjoyment of woods and waters, his more than pastoral or literary feeling that, however various the fables would allow him to be, 'l'amour' (as he was to write in one of the *Contes*) 'semble né pour les champs'.

In our day we have seen the familiar employed rather differently but to the same end of public acceptability by the Poet Laureate. La Fontaine borrowed and then adapted tales, or fables – for the most part – and supplied the poetry, whereas Sir John Betjeman has borrowed the poetry – for the most part – and floated his poems into acceptance on the back of long familiar, still acceptable, yet, *vis-à-vis* the poetic time he lives in, outmoded metric and melody. But then La Fontaine – see this time his preface to the first of the *Contes et Nouvelles* – was very clear that the poetry, 'the beauty and the grace', is in the poet's telling, not in what he tells.

If it is his poetry which matters most of all, it is all the same worth looking at La Fontaine's sources. Enumerated and examined, they show us that always rare welcome being, an educated poet, at work; a poet whose education tempers and tints his peculiarities and his subtleties. They show how inquisitive La Fontaine was, how indefatigable, when an end was in view; how he added to himself as poet by his reading and exploring, with no modern libraries and bibliographies to help him.

He draws most of all on Aesop, of course, piously setting at the head of his first collection a translation of the Byzantine legends which served as a biography of Aesop.

Phaedrus, whose fables are not all from Aesop, comes second. Some two dozen La Fontaine derived from an Italian humanist Laurentius Abstemius – from his Latin verse translations of Greek fables, published in Venice in 1495; and more than a dozen from the fables of Bidpai (Pilpay), which had been known in Europe since the thirteenth century. Indeed, obvious or less obvious, known or little known, there was hardly a fabulist, or collector of fables or adapter of fables or translator of fables, ancient or more or less modern, Italian or French, whom La Fontaine did not plunder in his way for at least one or two subjects; he also invented quite a few fables of his own.

At the start, it was perhaps Horace's versifying of a fable or two (Horace, in his *Satires*, gave him in particular his 'Town Rat and the Country Rat' – 1, 1x) which had suggested the undertaking, and even justified it.

At the very end, for the Twelfth Book, published in 1694 in his old age, La Fontaine was still casting around for clues, suggestions, subjects. He had drawn on other poets as well as fabulists, on Martial, Seneca, Regnier, Samuel Butler, and even on the Persian poet and moralist Sa'di. Lively still in his later manner, though feeling that his imagination had been enfeebled by the years, he ranged from the Norman poet Haudent and the Venetian verse fabulist Verdizotti, to the popular sixteenth-century stories of Gianfrancesco Straparola, and, for one fable, 'Le renard et les poulets d'Inde', **to** the *De anima brutorum* (1672) of the great English physician Thomas Willis, the identifier of diabetes (but then La Fontaine's curiosity stretched to science, and he had his learned scientific friends).

The world has taken the *Fables* rather no doubt as La Fontaine expected it would, not as he hoped it would, except in his own language community. Like the master-fables of Aesop, the fables of Phaedrus, the fables of Bidpai and the rest, La Fontaine's, retold, refashioned, have in their turn been translated into nearly every language, for their fabular content ('Ces fables', he says of all the fables of the ancient writers, introducing his own first collection of 1668, 'sont un tableau où chacun de nous se trouve dépeint'), for their dramatic entertaining worldliness and applicability, in

> Une ample comédie à cent actes divers,
> Et dont la scène est l'univers
> (v, 1);

for the pleasure, which seems built into us, of reading about animals who can talk, about lions, weasels, rabbits, frogs, oxen, rats, cats, dogs, wolves, monkeys, ducks and eagles and kites and above all the fox, acting their human parts and proverbs, or proverbial wisdom; on the long road – ultimate loss of poetry – to the brisk aesthetically obscene falsities of the Disney poultry yard and zoo.

But what happens to the poetry – when La Fontaine's is an especially fine and delicious case of the poetry existing in its own words? If we are not his countrymen, and are short in his language, the best we can do is read the most enjoyable and sympathetic translations we can find; and in my judgement the best are the ones by James Michie which follow, earthier and sharper than Marianne Moore's, and without the coyness into which Edward Marsh often collapsed. Then we need to set these good translations against as much as we can discern of the poetry of the originals.

Yet there are qualities we can detect at once, especially in the fables of Books I to VI, which are so fresh, so intimate, so able to unite poet and reader. We see at once a charming adequacy of means to end, a lack of what Coleridge meant by too-muchness, a perkiness which lacks the bad flavour of the word, not demeaning itself and never, or hardly ever, losing that friendliness which La Fontaine shows to us, and which we return to him (James Michie's versions are friendly in just that way). Directness is another engaging quality, no delay, no pause to show off. The fable, the poem, will direct us to its implication, or the situation, his openings, as often as not, being so active and faultless. We become immediate onlookers, for instance, in 'Le coche et la mouche' (VII, IX), where we might be watching from a sandbank:

> Dans un chemin montant, sablonneux, malaisé,
> Et de tous les côtés au soleil exposé,
>   Six forts chevaux tiraient un coche.
> Femmes, moine, vieillards, tout était descendu.
> L'attelage suait, soufflait, était rendu.

And then – 'Une mouche survient . . .' and the realism extends its conviction into the fable, into the horse-fly's remarks which follow.

We accept at once this rightness of every such scene or situation. Down comes a mountain torrent (VIII, XXIII), in two first lines:

> Avec grand bruit et grand fracas
> Un torrent tombait des montagnes.

We never doubt the knowledge so actively, so naturally on display, as when the master comes into the ox-shed out in the fields ('L'oeil du maître', IV, XXI):

> Qu'est-ce ci? dit-il à son monde.
> Je trouve bien peu d'herbe en tous ces râteliers.
> Cette litière est vieille; allez vite aux greniers.
> Je veux voir désormais vos bêtes mieux soignées.
> Que coûte-t-il d'ôter toutes ces araignées?
> Ne saurait-on ranger ces jougs et ces colliers?

And yet as a rule La Fontaine, with the authority of experience and of art, describes without description, the sparer the more vivid, the more affecting.

> Un pauvre bûcheron, tout couvert de ramée,
> Sous le faix du fagot aussi bien que des ans
> Gémissant et courbé marchait à pas pesants,
> Et tâchait de gagner sa chaumine enfumée

– isn't that (the opening of 'La mort et le bûcheron', I, XVI) as convincing, as spare, as affecting as a drawing or painting by Millet, two hundred years later, in which peasant and faggot seem one sad animal?

Of this analytic, conscious artist who considered the rôle and the possibilities of verse in general and especially in his own time, we can say, as he in turn said of Aesop, that 'son âme maintint toujours libre et indépendante de la fortune.' Wishing to please, his readers, he hoped and believed that they would like what he liked himself. Readers, he understood, wanted novelty and gaiety, to which he wasn't averse; by gaiety he did not mean the mirth which makes for laughter, 'but a certain charm, an agreeable air, which can be given to subjects of every kind, even the more serious ones.'

Brevity, structure, matters of style, choice of language, insertion of old among new, quick movement of *vers irrégulier* with those sudden short lines and that frequent suddenness of feminine rhyme which can create such point, such surprise, such fun, and make for almost conversational intimacy – La Fontaine was expert in them all. Had Mozart lived a hundred years earlier, he would have understood why Sainte-Beuve once called Mozart, for grace, lightness, and facility, 'the La Fontaine of music' (more tactful as it might have been to speak of La Fontaine, in those respects, as the Mozart of French verse).

He is the music-master at need; and here he moves into his 'magic', into that melodic depth which marks genius in poetry, defies inner translation, inevitably, and can be savoured entirely, we have to conclude, only by those who share a poet's language.

In the *Fables* it seems to be encountered most often in the first six books, in which the poems are so varied, and arranged so tactfully and diversely in their sequence. Later on La Fontaine does give some critics their excuse for feeling surfeited with the *Fables*: he does forego his devotion to brevity – 'qu'on peut fort bien appeler l'âme du conte' – lengthening and becoming a little preachy.

When he introduces his second collection, Books VII to XI, La Fontaine speaks of familiar, domestic strokes which he does not like to repeat: strokes of which he has not an infinite supply, and which, anyhow, are less fitted to his newer fables (he was departing more often from Aesop, though he did not desert him, and taking now to Bidpaï, among others). It is as if he had spent – and realized it – all he accumulated from the years of early love and of the woods and waters and solitude of Château-Thierry, and was afraid of the weakness of an overdraft. Poets age, and haven't an endless power of renewal.

At the end of one of his tales ('La Clochette', from *Contes et Nouvelles*), about the seduction of a cow-girl in the woods, La Fontaine, as if bored with its commonplace, suddenly reverts to his melodic self. 'O belles,' he warns young women, 'évitez'

> Le fond des bois et leur vaste silence

– a line out of keeping, yet of marvellous resonance, also a line which is much, incidentally, of France, and all of forests. It is into such visionary solitude that he introduces himself again and again in the *Fables*, ruthless and worldly as they are. Book I begins, Ant to Cicada, with the sharp voice of the headmistress, the ward sisters of this world, then finishes with the infinite vision of nature, time, life and death. 'Mais vous naissez,' says the Oak to the Reed, which feels the weight of the wren and survives the storm – 'le plus souvent'

> Sur les humides bords des royaume du vent

and it is the Oak which falls, whose head neighboured the sky,

> Et dont les pieds touchaient à l'empire des morts.

The grand lines multiply. In some of them La Fontaine seems to speak in his own voice almost as if no literature, ancient or modern, lay between himself and his experience. Sometimes he speaks through pastoralism –

> Le long d'un clair ruisseau buvait une colombe

– in its mode, yet still in his own voice. But then it is a common ignorance of poetry to put dismissively down to Virgil, Theocritus, Ovid, etc., to imitation, anything that such a poet as Ronsard or La Fontaine writes out of himself, yet through the classics. Ronsard's Bas-Vendômois and La Fontaine's country of the Marne exist within their classicism or pastoralism; and no one should fail to discern the authenticity of La Fontaine, when, for instance, in a late fable (the one – XI, IV – which he fashioned from Sa'di) he writes

> Solitude où je trouve une douceur secrète,
> Lieux que j'aimai toujours, ne pourrai-je jamais,
> Loin du monde et du bruit goûter l'ombre et le frais?
> O qui m'arrêtera sous vos sombres asiles,

or when, exercises of gallantry or no, this poet approaching sixty recalls

> J'ai quelquefois aimé; je n'aurais pas alors
> Contre le Louvre et ses trésors,
> Contre le firmament et sa voûte céleste,
> Changé les bois, changé les lieux
> Honorés par les pas, éclairés pas les yeux
> De l'aimable et jeune bergère
> Pour qui sous le fils de Cythère
> Je servis engagé par mes premiers serments

in a fable ('Les deux pigeons', IX, II) of which the last, famous line is

> Ai-je passé le temps d'aimer?

Such are the lines by which La Fontaine, who never wanted to grow old, who took a poor view of death – 'Ne viens jamais, ô mort' – seems still to his countrymen one of the greatest of their poets, and the one who is more French than the others.

After his death at last, in 1695, in his seventy-fifth year, his friend Maucroix mourned him as a very dear, very faithful comrade he had loved for more than fifty years, the most sincere and candid soul he had ever known – 'jamais déguisement' (which reminds me of Samuel Palmer's description of Blake as a man without a mask). 'I don't know,' Maucroix wrote, 'if he ever told a lie in his life.'

Add to that a passage in La Fontaine's *Les Amours de Psyché et de Cupidon*, in which, as Polyphile, who 'loved everything', he reads out a hymn to Volupté, lively, enjoyable Sensual Pleasure, begging her to lie with him:

> J'aime le jeu, l'amour, les livres, la musique,
> La ville et la campagne, enfin tout; il n'est rien
> Qui ne me soit souverain bien,
> Jusqu'au sombre plaisir d'un coeur mélancolique.

It is his autobiography, Volupté, 'la douce Volupté',

> qui fus jadis maîtresse
> Du plus bel esprit de la Grèce,

having come to him, and stayed with him.

GEOFFREY GRIGSON

TRANSLATOR'S NOTE: The *Fables* of La Fontaine were originally published in two collections, with an interval of ten years between. The first (1668), consisting of the first six books, had as its chief model Phaedrus, the Latin writer who versified the prose fables of the legendary Aesop. The second, which added six more books, had wider sources of inspiration, notably the Indian fabulist Bidpai, and is marked by greater metrical liberty and an element of meditative digression. I have tried to make my selection, a little over a quarter of all the *Fables*, representative, but it is inevitably biased towards those that are traditionally famous, those that tell a good story – and, it must be confessed, those that lent themselves more easily to translation. For readers who want to explore La Fontaine as a man and a highly original poet, I recommend *La Fontaine and His Friends* by Agnes Ethel Mackay (Garnstone Press, 1972).

LA FONTAINE: SELECTED FABLES

THE CICADA AND THE ANT

The cicada, having chirped her song
　　　All summer long,
　　Found herself bitterly deprived
　　When the north wind arrived –
　　Not a mouthful of worm or fly.
　　　Whereupon in her want
She rushed round to her neighbour the ant
　　　And begged her to supply
Some crumbs on loan to keep body and soul together
Till next spring. 'On my word as an animal
　　I swear,' she said, 'to repay
With interest before the harvest ends.'
Of the ant's few faults the minimal
　　　Is that she never lends.
'What were you doing during the hot weather?'
She asked the importunate insect.
　　　'With all respect,
　　　I was singing night and day
For the pleasure of anyone whom chance
　　　Sent my way.'
　　　　'Singing, did you say?
I'm delighted to hear it. Now you can dance!'

FABLE II

THE CROW AND THE FOX

Mr Crow, perched in a tree, held in his beak
    A piece of cheese.
Mr Fox, attracted by the smell,
    Began to speak
    In terms roughly like these:
    'Hullo!
I mean, good morning, honourable Crow,
    You look uncommonly well,
Indeed you look a veritable Romeo.
Honestly, if it were not for one thing
You would be the phoenix of our woodland birds:
Your feathers are gorgeous – but how well can you sing?'
    At these words
The crow, beside himself with pleasure,
Opened his big mouth to show off, and dropped his treasure.
The fox snapped it up in a trice,
Remarking: 'My dear sir, learn the hard way
    That all flatterers live
At the expense of those with a credulous ear to give –

A lesson cheap, surely, at the price
    Of your lost cheese-slice.'
    Mortified and confused,
The crow vowed (rather late in the day)
Never again to be so abused.

FABLE III

THE FROG WHO WANTED TO BE AS BIG AS THE OX

A frog saw an ox: in his eyes
A huge and handsome figure.
He, who was no bigger
Than an egg from top to toe,
In envy stretched and strained in an effort to blow
Himself up to the same size.
'Just watch me closely, Sis.
Tell me, am I large enough?
Have I got there yet?' 'No.' More huff and puff.
'Well, look at me now!' Another 'No'.
'Then what about this?'
'You've still a long way to go.'
At which the poor frog, overloaded
With wind and vanity, exploded.

The world is full of men as foolish as that.
The tradesman wants to build like an aristocrat.
The petty prince employs
Ambassadors; the marquess errand-boys.

FABLE IV

THE TWO MULES

Two mules were travelling the same road,
One carrying money to pay the salt-tax,
    The other grain-sacks.
The leader, proud of his important load –
He wouldn't have wanted it lighter for anything –
    Was putting on speed
    And making his mule-bells ring
When bandits came up, who, being in need
    Of money, aimed their attack
At the one with the cash for the tax on salt,
Seized his bridle and brought him to a halt.
    The mule fought back
But was clubbed and stabbed. 'Is this what I was led
To expect from my masters?' he said
    With a bitter sigh.
'The mule behind me gets off scot-free
While I'm done for, left here to die!'
    'Friend,' said the other mule,
    'It's not always the rule
That it pays to be in the service of the rich.
If you worked for a mere miller, like me,
You wouldn't be groaning in that ditch.'

FABLE VI

THE HEIFER, THE NANNY-GOAT
AND THE SHEEP IN PARTNERSHIP WITH THE LION

The heifer, the nanny-goat and the sheep
Formed a partnership in the days of old
With the haughty lion, the local boss,
    By which they agreed to hold
Everything in common and to keep
A joint account of profit or of loss.
      One day a stag got snared
In the nets of the goat. She at once sent word
To her associates, and they all conferred.
Counting up on his claws, the lion declared:
    'Our catch has to be shared
Among us four.' Then, carving up the game
Into four quarters, he laid claim
To the first on the grounds that he was a lord:
    'I'm entitled to award
This chunk to myself because Lion is my name.'
    Not a murmur of protest was heard.
    'The second portion,' he averred,
    'Must likewise belong
To me by right – the right, of course, of the strong.
As the bravest of us I am owed the third.
And if any of you touches the last lot,
    She'll be strangled on the spot!'

FABLE IX

THE TOWN RAT AND THE COUNTRY RAT

Town Rat once graciously
Asked Country Rat to dine
On ortolans left over
By the household. On a fine

Turkish cloth the plates
And knives and forks were laid.
I leave you to imagine
How merry the two friends made.

It was a handsome spread,
All that a rat could wish.
Yet someone marred the mood
Half-way through the main dish.

Their ears picked up a sound
At the dining-room door. Cat!
Town Rat bolted for cover,
Followed by Country Rat.

The scratching ceased, the prowler
Moved off. At once the host
Led his friend back to the field:
'Now let's finish our roast.'

'That's enough, thanks,' said the other.
'Tomorrow you'll be my guest.
It's not that I'm critical of
The food – you served the best.

But at home I eat in peace,
And nobody interrupts.
Goodbye, then. And to hell
With pleasure that fear corrupts!'

FABLE X

THE WOLF AND THE LAMB

Might is right: the verdict goes to the strong.
To prove the point won't take me very long.

    A lamb was once drinking
From a clear stream when a foraging wolf came slinking
    Out of the woods, drawn to that quarter
    Of the countryside by hunger.
    'How dare you muddy my drinking water!'
    Said the beast of prey in anger.
'You shall be punished for your insolence.'
    'Your Majesty,' answered the lamb,
'I beg you not to be angry but to think
    Calmly about it. Here I am,
    Relieving my throat's dryness
At least twenty yards downstream from your Highness,
    And in consequence
    I cannot be in the least
    Guilty of sullying your royal drink.'
    'But you are,' said the pitiless beast.
'Besides, I know you spoke ill of me last year.'
'How could I have done? I wasn't even here,'

The lamb replied. 'I'm still at the teat of my mother.'
'If it wasn't you, it must have been your brother.'
'I haven't got one.' 'Well, then, one of you sheep;
For you and your shepherds and damned dogs keep
Making it harder and harder for me to eat.
But now revenge is mine – and revenge is sweet!'
Whereupon he dragged the lamb deep
Into the forest and had his meal.
There was no right of appeal.

FABLE XVIII

THE FOX AND THE STORK

One day Mr Fox decided to fork out
And invite old Mrs Stork out.
The dinner wasn't elaborate –
     Being habitually mean,
He didn't go in for *haute cuisine* –
In fact it consisted of a shallow plate
     Of thin gruel.
     Within a minute
Our joker had lapped his plate clean;
Meanwhile his guest, fishing away with her beak,
     Got not a morsel in it.
To pay him back for this cruel
Practical joke, the stork invited
The fox to dinner the following week.
     'I should be delighted,'
     He replied;
'When it comes to friends I never stand upon pride.'
Punctually on the day he ran
To his hostess's house and at once began
Praising everything: 'What taste! What chic!
And the food – done just to a turn!'
Then sat down with a hearty appetite

(Foxes are always ready to eat)
And savoured the delicious smell of meat.
It was minced meat and served – to serve him right! –
In a long-necked, narrow-mouthed urn.

      The stork, easily stooping,
      Enjoyed her fill
      With her long bill;
His snout, though, being the wrong shape and size,
      He had to return to his den
Empty-bellied, tail dragging, ears drooping,
As red in the face as a fox who's been caught by a hen.

      Watch out, you foxes among men –
      To you my tale applies!

FABLE XIX

THE BOY AND THE SCHOOLMASTER

This fable aims to paint a picture
Of a fool and a foolish moral lecture.

A young boy, playing on the bank
Of the Seine, fell in and nearly sank.
But Heaven had providentially
Positioned there a willow-tree
Whose weeping branches overhung
The water, and to which he clung.
A schoolmaster was passing by.
Arrested by the juvenile's cry
Of 'Help! I think I'm going to drown!'
He seized the chance to dress him down
In solemn tones (not the best place
Or time for words): 'Baboon! Scapegrace!
Look what a mess you've landed in!
To think I have to discipline
Rascals like you, boy! I could weep
For parents duty-bound to keep
A ceaseless supervising eye
On such unteachable *canaille*.

Poor people! What a life!' Whereat
He hauled to land the erring brat.

I level here the finger of blame
At more folk than you might surmise.
Prudes, windbags, pedants, recognize
Yourselves as targets of my aim:
Three categories which comprise
Vast numbers of that breed of pest
Whom God apparently has blessed.
In all affairs they only think
Of how to exercise their breath.
My friend, you snatch me from disaster's brink
And then proceed to lecture me to death!

FABLE XX

THE COCK AND THE PEARL

A cock, scratching around,
Finding a pearl on the ground,
Took it along to swap
At the nearest jeweller's shop:
'I think it's very striking,
But millet's more to my liking.'

An ignoramus took
An old manuscript book
Left to him in a will
To his neighbour the bibliophile:
'I think it's very fine,
But money's more in my line.'

FABLE XXII

THE OAK AND THE REED

One day the oak said to the reed:
'You have good cause indeed
To accuse Nature of being unkind.
To you a wren must seem
An intolerable burden, and the least puff of wind
That chances to wrinkle the face of the stream
Forces your head low; whereas I,
Huge as a Caucasian peak, defy
Not only the sun's glare, but the worst the weather can do.
What seems a breeze to me is a gale for you.
Had you been born in the lee of my leaf-sheltered ground,
You would have suffered less, I should have kept you warm;
But you reeds are usually found
On the moist borders of the kingdom of the storm.
It strikes me that to you Nature has been unfair.'
'Your pity,' the plant replied, 'springs from a kind heart.
But please don't be anxious on my part.
Your fear of the winds ought to be greater than mine.
I bend, but I never break. You, till now, have been able to bear
Their fearful buffets without flexing your spine.

But let us wait and see.' Even as he spoke,
From the horizon's nethermost gloom
The worst storm the north had ever bred in its womb
     Furiously awoke.
The tree stood firm, the reed began to bend.
The wind redoubled its efforts to blow –
     So much so
     That in the end
It uprooted the one that had touched the sky with its head,
But whose feet reached to the region of the dead.

FABLE VII

THE BITCH AND HER FRIEND

Expecting a large litter any minute
And having nowhere to lie in for labour,
A bitch finally coaxed her neighbour
Into offering the loan of her own hut.
Having made herself comfortable in it,
When in due course her friend
Returned she asked her to extend
The time by two weeks more. Her pups, she pleaded,
Were late in coming and besides . . . To cut
My story short, she succeeded.
The fortnight's grace being over
And the friend arriving to recover
Her roof, her room and her bed,
This time, baring her teeth, the bitch said:
'Of course my family and I
Won't stay a moment longer –
That is, if you can throw us out. Just try!'
(By now the puppies had grown stronger.)

One invariably regrets
Loans to unpleasant people. To reclaim those debts
You have to resort to threats,
To the law, to physical force as well.
Give them an inch and they take an ell.

FABLE IX

THE LION AND THE GNAT

'Buzz off, you miserable insect! Little turd!'
    The gnat, thus addressed,
Declared war on the lion. 'Do you suppose
That I'm awed, even impressed
By your royal title? The ox is just as large
And strong as you, yet I lead him by the nose.'
Whereupon, as good as his word,
Both trumpeter and hero of his charge,
    He sounded the attack.
Manoeuvring for room at first, he took
His time, then dived on his opponent's back
And stung the lion till he was almost crazed.
He foamed at the mouth, his eyes blazed,
He roared so loud that the neighbourhood shook
    And everyone round about,
      Terrified, hid.
All the work of a mere ephemerid!
In the back, on the muzzle, right up his snout,
In a hundred places the gnat made him itch
Until his rage reached such a pitch
That gleefully his invisible conqueror saw
    That he had no need

Of tooth or claw
To make his maddened enemy bleed,
For the wretched beast, rending his own skin,
Lashing his flanks with his tail, flailing
The air in a frenzy, strength and fury failing,
    At last collapsed, all in.
Covered with glory, once more to the sound
Of his own trumpet, the gnat
Retired victorious from the fray
And bustled off to buzz the news around.
    On the way
He ran into a spider's web – and that was that!

    What can this story teach us?
    I see a double lesson here:
First, that among our enemies those we should fear
The most are often the puniest creatures;
Second, that he who has just fought clear
Of a great danger may easily run
Straight to his death in a lesser one.

FABLE X

THE DONKEY LOADED WITH SPONGES
AND THE DONKEY LOADED WITH SALT

Our hero, the donkey-driver, leads
    Two gallant, droop-eared steeds
In the style of a Roman emperor, right hand
    Grasping his switch like a mace.
One, carrying sponges, sets a courier's pace;
The other, on unwilling legs,
    Walks, as they say, on eggs,
His load being salt. This merry band,
Up hill, down dale, by many a track,
At last came to a ford which blocked their way.
The man, who made the crossing every day,
Mounted the donkey with the sponges' back
And dealt the other's rump a whack,
    Who, eager to have his head,
Dashed forward, fell down a hole in the stream-bed,
Came up, climbed out and gave his friends the slip –
    For by the end of his dip
    His salt-load had all melted,
So that his shoulders hardly felt it.
Following his lead as blindly as a sheep,

At once his brother plunges
      After him neck-deep
Into the stream, where, wallowing,
All of them do a vast amount of swallowing,
Driver and beast competing with the sponges.
      In fact these last
      Absorb so much so fast
That, sinking under the extra weight,
The animal can't struggle back to land.
Expecting any moment to be drowned,
The donkey-man throws his arms around
His ass's neck and in that state
Is rescued by a helping hand.
Whose it was is neither here nor there:
I'm only showing we must all take care
Never to get in a scrape like that.
That's the point I've been driving at.

FABLE XI

THE LION AND THE RAT

In this world we must do our best
    To oblige others; for we all
    Occasionally have need to call
On the services of the weak and small.
    This truth two fables attest:
Indeed proofs of all such truths abound.

Rashly popping from a hole in the ground,
A rat came up between a lion's paws.
The king of beasts, sheathing his claws,
In this instance showed his royal nature
    And spared the little creature.
The kindness wasn't wasted. . . . But a rat
    Paying a lion back a debt –
    Could anyone credit that?
And yet it happened. On the fringe of the jungle
The same lion was later caught in a net
Which all his roars were powerless to untangle.
    Up ran Sir Rat and set
To work with his teeth, gnawing and fretting,
Till, mesh by mesh, he'd unpicked all the netting.

Patience and perseverance at length
Accomplish more than anger and brute strength.

FABLE XII

THE PIGEON AND THE ANT

My other example features
Rather smaller creatures.

A pigeon was drinking
From the clear waters of a brook
When an ant, leaning over the bank,
Fell in. Seeing it struggling hard but sinking
In that sea, the kind-natured pigeon took
Instant action: she threw a blade of grass in
Which served it as a sort of plank
To crawl back to dry land.
Saved! Soon a villager, passing
Noiselessly in bare feet,
Who happened to have a crossbow in his hand,
Caught sight of Venus's bird.
At once he saw her simmering in the pot
And himself relishing the meat.
Just as he took aim to bring down his meal
The ant stung him in the heel.
The fellow jerked his head – the pigeon heard,
Rose and was out of range of a shot.
The bumpkin's supper vanished with her flight.
No cheap pigeon-pie tonight!

FABLE XIV

THE HARE AND THE FROGS

A hare was brooding in his lair.
(What else is there to do in a lair for a hare?)
Gnawed by anxiety, deep in neurotic despair,
    This one was thinking:
'Creatures by nature timid and shrinking
    Lead a miserable existence.
    They can't digest their food
    So that it does them good.
For them no pleasure's pure – there's always a threat in the distance.
That's how I live. My damned nerves keep
    My eyes open even when I sleep.
    Some bright person no doubt
    Will say: "Why not simply *decide*
    Not to be terrified?"
    Yes, but can fear cast *itself* out?
Yet even men, I bet, feel just as afraid.'
So he considered the problem – and stayed
Worried and jumpy and wide-awake:
A breath of wind, a shadow, a nothing made
    This melancholy hare
    Feverishly shake.
    In the middle of his daymare

He heard a rustle. Had it been a gun
Going off he couldn't have run
Faster back to his form.
As he fled past a pond a swarm
Of frogs erupted – frogs leaping helter-skelter,
Frogs diving for shelter,
Frogs frantic everywhere!
'Aha,' thought he,
'Now I'm doing what others have done to me.
I frightened them simply by being there,
I sent the camp scrambling to panic stations!
I can't believe it, I'm the scourge of nations,
I'm Attila the Hun!
But from what does my new-found courage derive?
I realize now there's not a coward alive
Who can't find an even bigger one.'

FABLE XV

THE ROOSTER AND THE FOX

A shrewd, wily old rooster
Was keeping look-out on a bough
When a fox, in the nicest voice he could muster,
Addressed him: 'Brother,
We are no longer at war with each other:
I've come to announce that it's peace now,
Total peace! Descend and accept my embrace.
But for goodness' sake
Don't keep me waiting – today I'm in a hurry,
With twenty different calls to make.
From now on you and your race
Can go about your business free of worry –
We shall treat you as brothers. Let us light
Jubilee bonfires tonight.
Meanwhile come and receive a fraternal kiss.'
'My friend,' the rooster replied, 'I couldn't have heard
Better or more welcome news than this.
Peace is a wonderful word,
And to me it's a double delight
To hear it from you. But wait!
I see two hounds – they must be envoys sent
Expressly to attend this great event.

They'll be here in a moment, to judge by their pace.
Then I'll get down and we can all four embrace.'
'Goodbye,' said the fox. 'I've a long day ahead.
      We'll have to celebrate
      Tomorrow, or the day after. . . .'
      Whereupon, sick
      At the failure of his trick,
That gentleman hitched his trousers up and fled.
The old cock watched his panicky retreat
      With silent laughter;
      For the pleasure is twice as sweet
      When you cheat a cheat.

FABLE XVII

THE PEACOCK WHO COMPLAINED TO JUNO

The peacock once complained to Juno.
'Goddess,' he was saying, 'you know
What good reason I have to moan and groan.
The voice you've made peculiarly my own
    Is abhorrent to all nature,
Whereas the nightingale, that puny creature,
Has a song so clear and ravishing
That he's the star attraction of the spring.'
    Angrily Juno replied:
'Envious bird, you should keep quiet!
    You from whose shoulders
    Hangs such an iridescent riot
Of silken colour, you who strut in the pride
    Of your magnificent tail
That seems a jeweller's showcase to beholders –
Are *you* jealous of the nightingale?
Is there a bird under the sky
With your ability to delight the eye?
No animal is blessed with all the talents.
We gods, in giving, have preserved a balance:
Some of you were created big and strong;
The eagle's fierce, the falcon swift;

The raven's role is storm-divining,
The crow's to warn men of impending doom.
    Each is content with the gift
    Of his own song.
    So stop whining,
Or I'll strip you bare of every gorgeous plume!'

THE MILLER, HIS SON AND THE DONKEY

Art being our inheritance, we're in debt
To ancient Greece for the fable-form; and yet
The field has not been harvested so clean
That late arrivers can't find ears to glean,
For the world of fiction's full of virgin spaces,
And every day our authors plant new places.
Here's a neat, striking story which was told
To the up-and-coming Racan by the old
Poet Malherbe. Disciples of Apollo,
Heirs of the lyre of Horace, eager to follow
And equal him, our masters in a word,
These two, meeting one day un-overheard,
Shared their most intimate thoughts. Racan began:
'I beg you, my dear sir, since you're a man
Who must know life profoundly, having passed
Through all its seven ages but the last,
Whose eye nothing escapes – tell me, what goal
Should I set myself? It's time I searched my soul.
You know my circumstances, means and birth
And what, if anything, my talent's worth.

Should I settle in the provinces? Become
A court follower? Beat the soldier's drum?
All life consists of bitterness and charms:
War has its pleasures, marriage its alarms.
If I had only myself to please, I'd know;
But there are my friends, the court, the world, and so. . . .'
'What! Please them all!' Malherbe exclaimed. 'Absurd!
Until you've heard this tale judgement's deferred:

I've read somewhere of a miller and his son,
An old man and a boy – not a little one
But about fifteen if memory serves me well –
Who were going one fine market-day to sell
Their donkey. So that he'd get there in good trim
And fetch a better price they hobbled him
And carried him on a pole, slung in mid-air
Like a chandelier. What a pathetic pair
Of rustic fools! The first person who saw
The trio burst into a loud guffaw.
"What comedy are this troupe going to act
In the next village?" he enquired. "In fact,
Which of the three is the real ass, I wonder?"
At this the miller recognized his blunder,
Set the beast on his feet and urged him up the road.
The ass, who'd much enjoyed his previous mode
Of travel, hee-hawed "Nay!" Paying no heed,
The father told his son to ride and lead.
Soon they met three rich merchants, who were appalled
By the spectacle. "Whoa there!" the eldest called
At the top of his voice. "Get down – yes, you, the lad
With the grey-haired lackey. Really, it's too bad!
Your job's to walk, it's the old chap who should ride."
"Your wish, gentlemen, shall be satisfied,"

The miller said. At once his son got down
And he took his place in the saddle. Nearer town
Three girls passed. "Shame!" one shouted. "It's all wrong
For the young boy to have to limp along
While that buffoon sprawls like a calf up there
As smug as an old bishop on his chair!"
"At my age I can hardly be called calf,"
Said the miller. "Shove off, girl, don't make me laugh."
But after a brisk exchange of jeers and chaff
He changed his mind and put his son on the croup
Behind him. Thirty yards on, a third group
Of travellers had some fresh comments to make:
"They must be out of their minds. That beast can't take
Any more – he'll drop down dead at the next blow!
What a load for the poor old moke! You'd think they'd show
Some pity for a friend who's served them well.
I bet they're heading for the fair to sell
The hide." "Dear God," groaned the miller, "what a life!
To try to please the whole world and his wife
Is a daft thing to do. Still, let's see whether
We can solve this somehow." They got down together
And the ass walked grandly on a quarter-mile
Till somebody called out: "Is this the style
Nowadays – the donkey strolls and the miller trudges?
Did God mean beasts or masters to be drudges?
Wasting good shoe-leather to save an ass!
Why don't they keep the creature behind glass?
This is the opposite of Nicholas
In the old song, who went to see his lass
Mounted upon his donkey. Here I see
Three fine donkeys!" "All right, I agree,
I'm an ass," said the miller. "Very well, from today,
Whether the world has anything to say

Or nothing, I shall go my own sweet way
Just like an ass, ignoring blame or praise."
And so he did, and prospered all his days.

As for you, Racan, whether you plan
To follow Love or Mars or some great man,
Travel hectically or lead a quiet life
In the provinces, take, or not take, a wife,
Become an abbot, functionary, politician,
     Whatever your position
     There's no way out –
    You'll be unkindly talked about!'

FABLE IV

THE FROGS WHO ASKED FOR A KING

The frog nation, becoming bored
With democracy, raised such a fractious cry
That Jupiter appointed them an overlord.
The king who came down was far from being harsh;
Yet he made such a noise when he fell from the sky
    That the people of the marsh
    Rushed to hide themselves in the pools,
    In the reeds and rushes, in every nook
    Of their froggy bog,
    Without for a long time daring to face
    This strange giant. In fact it was a log
That had made the awesome splash. The first frog
    Who was daring enough to take a look
    Quitted his hiding place
    And swam up, trembling in every limb.
Another followed the first, a third followed him,
    Until finally a whole swarm,
    Getting cheekier and bolder,
Actually hopped on their monarch's shoulder,
Without a murmur of protest from the inert form
Of the old chap. Before long the frogs were clamouring:
    'We want an active king!'
    By now nearly out of his mind

With annoyance, Jupiter sent them a crane,
Who breakfasted and lunched and dined
On frogs whenever he felt inclined.
And still the frogs continued to complain.
This time Jupiter told them flat:
'Don't be silly. Do you think that my decrees
Can be repealed just as frogs please?
To start with, you should have kept
Your own government. Failing to do that,
You should have been content to accept
Your first king, who was amiable and kind.
    Learn to be grateful
    For the one you have – or you may find
    The next king far more hateful.'

FABLE V

THE FOX AND THE GOAT

Captain Fox, past master of every craft,
Was out with his friend the long-horned billy-goat,
Who never could see beyond his nose's end.
    The heat forced them to descend
    Down a deep well-shaft
    In order to relieve a dry throat.
When each had thoroughly quenched his thirst,
The fox said: 'What do we do now, friend?
    Life's not all about
    Drinking, we've got to get out.
Put your forelegs up, set your horns against the wall
And make a sort of ladder for me. First
I'll climb on your back, then I'll stand up
On your long horns, jump out and give you a hand-up.'
'By my beard,' said the goat, 'you're right! Upon my soul,
    I do admire people who are clever.
    I know I should never
Have solved the problem on my own.' And so,
    Leaving his friend below,
    The fox climbed out of the hole
And delivered a fine sermon to extol

The virtues of patience. 'If only,' he said,
'Heaven had put as many brains in your head
        As it did hairs on your chin,
You would never so rashly have clambered in.
        So here am I
        And there are you. Well, now try
Your damnedest to get yourself out. But I must fly –
        I can't stand here and chatter,
        I have an urgent matter
        To attend to. Goodbye.'

        Whatever you do,
        Keep the end of the business in view.

FABLE VII

THE DRUNKARD AND HIS WIFE

Every man has his vice, and without fail
    Returns to it: neither disgrace
    Nor fear can cure it. Apropos,
    I am reminded of a tale,
For I never speak unless I show
Some good example to support my case.

A slave of Bacchus was ruining his health,
His mental faculties and his purse.
(These boozers don't go half the course
Before they've squandered all their wealth.)
    One day, after he'd drowned
His senses in a bottle of the grape,
    His wife, by way of a jape,
Shut him up in a vault. There, underground,
The fumes of the new wine went to work,
Slowly fermenting. Waking with a jerk,
He saw Death's apparatus all around,
Down to the tapers and the winding-sheet.
    'Hullo, what's this?' he asked.
'Has my wife become a widow?' She, by his feet,

Dressed as the Fury Alecto, suitably masked,
Advanced towards the bier and offered her 'dead'
Husband some gruel hot enough for Satan.
By now confirmed in his suspicion
That he was one of Lucifer's damned legions,
     He asked the apparition:
     'Who are you?' 'I,' she said
     In an appropriate voice of doom,
'Am the caterer of the infernal regions.
My job is to bring food and wait on
The inmates of the dark and dreary tomb.'
     Without pausing to think,
He groaned: 'What! Nothing to drink?'

FABLE IX

THE WOLF AND THE STORK

Wolves are gluttonous feeders.
    This wolf, readers,
Gobbled so fast that a bone got stuck in his craw
    And he thought he was going to die.
Luckily for him a stork, passing by,
Seeing him signalling and silently choking,
Ran up and performed an emergency operation.
Having removed the bone with her beak, she asked for remuneration.
'Remuneration? My good woman, you must be joking.
    Don't be absurd.
Isn't it enough that you managed to withdraw
Your neck unbitten from my jaw?
    Go away, ungrateful bird –
And never again come within reach of my paw!'

FABLE X

THE LION HUMBLED BY MAN

A canvas was once shown
In which the painter had depicted a huge lion and one lone
Hunter subduing it:
A source of great human pride to the people viewing it,
Until a passing lion silenced their self-applause.
'It's obvious enough,' he said,
'That in this case the victory is yours.
But you've been misled
By the artist, who is free to invent anything that comes into his head.
If my brothers knew how to paint, it would be another story:
Lions would win all the glory!'

FABLE XI

THE FOX AND THE GRAPES

A starving fox – a Gascon, Normans claim,
But Gascons say a Norman – saw a cluster
Of luscious-looking grapes of purplish lustre
Dangling above him on a trellis-frame.
He would have dearly liked them for his lunch,
But when he tried and failed to reach the bunch:
'Ah well, it's more than likely they're not sweet –
    Good only for green fools to eat!'

Wasn't he wise to say they were unripe
    Rather than whine and gripe?

FABLE XIV

THE LION IN HIS OLD AGE

The lion, whom all the forest fears,
    Overburdened by years
And mourning his great prowess of the past,
    Was attacked at last
By his own subjects, who as he grew older
    Became bolder and bolder.
The horse approached and gave him a kick,
    The wolf a nip with his teeth,
    The ox a gore with his horn.
    The mortally sick,
    Miserable, age-worn
Lion could scarcely muster a roar
And uncomplainingly awaited death.
But when he saw the donkey at his door,
    He was moved to exclaim:
    'No, this is too much!
I'm ready to die, but to endure your touch
Would be to die a second death – of shame!'

FABLE II

THE SHEPHERD AND THE SEA

For many years a shepherd by the sea
      Had lived care-free
On the profit from his flock, which though not great
    Was regular at any rate.
At last the rich bales landed on the shore
    Proved so dazzling a bait
That he sold his flock and bought a share in a ship.
His new investment on its maiden trip
      Split on a rock
And the owner was reduced to sheep once more.
      No longer, as before,
A master shepherd with his own fine flock
Beside the sea, he who'd been known
As happy Thyrsis or brave Corydon
      Became plain Jack.
Time passed, he made some money and bought back
Some of the animals he'd sold,
And on one of those days when the winds hold
Their breath and allow vessels to glide
      Gently to land he cried:

'Are you greedy for money, sisters of the brine?
Tempt someone else. By God, you shan't have mine!'

      This isn't just a fanciful tale.
      I've tried to demonstrate
      What all experience proves is true:
      That a penny paid on the nail
Is worth much more than fivepence out of view,
That we should rest contented with our fate
      And shut our ears and eyes
To what ambition and the sea advise.
For one man she makes rich ten thousand come to grief.
      The sea offers us wonders,
      Eldorados, Golcondas;
Trust her – and you meet pirates, storms, a reef!

FABLE V

THE DONKEY AND THE LITTLE DOG

Never, if you've a talent, force the pace,
Or all you do will lack the charm of grace.
   However hard he tries, a peasant
   Can't pass for a man about town.
Few men on whom the cherishing gods look down
Are born with the natural gift of being pleasant.
It's a point people shouldn't press –
   That is, unless
They want to be like the donkey in the fable
   Who, to bind himself faster
   To the affections of his master,
   Tried to embrace him at table.
The beast had said to himself: 'It makes me sick
That just because he's small and sweet
   Dog should enjoy a life
As a friend and equal of Sir and his wife,
Whereas all I get is stick.
   Am I only fit to beat?
What does Dog do? Lifts paw, gets kiss.

   If it's as simple as that
   Why shouldn't I earn a pat
   As readily as the pup?'
After his well-thought-out analysis,
Seeing his master merry at a meal
   He came galumphing up,
   Lifted a gnarled old hoof
And laid it lovingly against Sir's chin,
Adding to this rash act, for extra appeal,
His musical equivalent of 'Woof!'
   'What a caress! Ouch, my skin!
   What an ear-splitting bray!
   Hey, donkey-boy, hey!'
In ran Jack with his stick and led away
An ass whose manners had been mended.
   Our comedy is ended.

FABLE IX

THE JAY DRESSED UP IN THE PEACOCK'S FEATHERS

Finding a peacock moulting, a jay snatched
Some of the feathers, which he then attached
To his own body. Fraudulently adorned,
      He was soon pluming
Himself among the peacocks and assuming
      The airs of a most important bird.
His disguise was seen through, for he looked absurd.
Teased, ridiculed, hissed at, utterly scorned,
He was plucked by the cockbirds, horribly, to the skin.
When he fled for refuge back to his own kin,
      Even the jays refused to let him in.

There are plenty of two-legged birds like these,
Dressed in plumes that are borrowed and not earned.
      Plagiarism is the name
      Of that particular game.
I'll say no more: I've no wish to displease
      Popinjays who put on airs;
      Besides, I'm not concerned
      With literary affairs.

FABLE X

THE CAMEL AND THE FLOATING STICKS

The first man who saw a camel fled;
The second ventured within distance;
The third dared slip a halter round its head.
    Familiarity in this existence
Makes all things tame, for what may seem
Terrible or bizarre, when once our eyes
    Have had time to acclimatize,
Becomes quite commonplace. Since I'm on this theme,
I've heard of sentinels posted by the shore
Who, spotting something far-away afloat,
        Couldn't resist the shout:
        'A sail! A sail!
        A mighty man-of-war!'
Five minutes later it's a packet-boat,
And then a skiff, and then a bale,
And finally some sticks bobbing about.

      I know of plenty such
      To whom this story applies –
People whom distance magnifies,
Who, close to, don't amount to much.

THE MISER WHO LOST HIS HOARD

Use, and use only, gives possession.
   I ask those people whose obsession
Is saving, hiding, heaping money in stacks,
What advantage have they which their neighbour lacks?
Diogenes, dead and buried in his grave,
Is as well off, for misers, whatever they save,
Live like dogs, as he did. The man with his hoard
     Whom Aesop mentions will afford
     An illustration of my theme.

     This miserable wretch, whose dream
Was immortal life to relish his wealth slowly
(He was possessed by *it*, not the other way round),
Had buried a huge sum underground,
And his heart with it, for his sole pleasure
     Was brooding on it night and day,
        Devoting himself wholly
To the religion of his sacred treasure.
Coming or going, eating or drinking,
You would be lucky to catch him thinking
Of anything but the place where the gold lay.
So often did he hover round the spot

That an observant ditcher,
Suspecting that his spade might make him richer,
Quietly removed the lot.
When our friend came back to find an eggless nest
He burst into tears – picture him groaning, sighing,
Tearing his hair, beating his breast!
A passer-by asked him why he was crying.
'Somebody's stolen my treasure,' wailed the miser.
'Your treasure, did you say? Where was it, then?'
'Right by that stone.' 'Good Lord, are we at war
That you should have had to carry it that far
To conceal it? Wouldn't you have been wiser
To have kept it at home in your den
Ready to hand for the daily occasions when –'
'Ready to hand? Heaven forbid! Do you suppose
That money returns at the same rate as it goes?
I never used to touch it.' 'Pray, then, explain
Why, my dear sir, you're in such evident pain
Over losing what you never used to touch.
Bury a stone there – it's worth just as much!'

FABLE II

THE CLAY POT AND THE IRON POT

Said the iron to the clay pot:
'Let's see the world together.'
'If you don't mind, I'd rather not,'
Said the other. 'I'm not sure whether
I would be wise to forsake
My corner of the ingle –
After all, it would only take
The slightest shock, one single
Accident to shatter
My body irrevocably.
But for you who are made of matter
Tougher than mine, I can see
No reason to stay inside.'
'But I'll be your bodyguard,'
The iron pot replied.
'If we happen to meet some hard
Impediment on our way
I'll stand between you and harm
As a buffer.' The pot of clay
Was persuaded. Arm in arm,

Brother escorting brother,
As best they could they set off
Six-leggedly, knocking each other
At the least stumble or cough.
The clay pot was bound to suffer.
Within a hundred yards
His bodyguard and buffer
Had smashed him into shards.
He had only himself to blame.

In life we observe the same.
One should only associate
With equals. He who does not
Is sure to suffer the fate
Of the vulnerable pot.

FABLE III

THE LITTLE FISH AND THE ANGLER

A little fish will grow,
Providing that God gives it time to, fatter;
But to let a tiddler go
And wait for that to happen in my view
Is a silly thing to do.
To catch fish twice isn't a simple matter.

One day a carp, still very young and small,
Was caught by an angler on the riverside.
'Well,' said the man, examining his haul,
'Everything counts. There's a delicious meal
Building up here. We'll pop it in our creel.'
The poor carp in his squeaky fashion cried:
'What are you going to do with me? For you
Half a mouthful's all I can provide.
Let me grow up, and by and by
I'll see to it that I'm caught
By you again, and then I'm sure to be bought
By some greedy tax-man from the Revenue
For a good price. If not, you'll have to try
To catch a hundred other fish
Of my size to make up a dish.

Some dish! Trust me, it'll be a paltry feast.'
    'Paltry? So be it,' said the man.
'My fine and fishy friend, though you can preach
        As well as any priest,
        For all your powers of speech
Tonight you end up in my frying-pan.'

A bird in the hand is reckoned
Worth two that you haven't yet shot.
The first bag's certain, the second
        Is not.

FABLE VI

THE OLD WOMAN AND THE TWO SERVANT-GIRLS

There was an old woman with two servant-girls
Who were such excellent spinners
That the three Fates were amateurs, mere beginners
Compared with them. Her one daily concern
Was to assign them a work-load.
As soon as Tethys, sister of the Ocean,
Had roused Apollo of the golden curls,
      Wheels started to turn,
        Spindles whirred into motion;
All day and half the night, non-stop,
They were made to spin till they were fit to drop.
The moment Dawn had got his team on the road,
      As I've just said,
A scrawny cock, horribly punctual, crowed
And, scrawnier still, the crone threw on a skirt
(A frightful garment stiff with dirt),
Lit an old lamp and ran straight to the bed
Where her two maids, with all their might,
With all their night-starved appetite,
Were sleeping deeply. One half-opened an eye,
One stretched an arm, and with concerted spite,
Through gritted teeth, both swore:

'You bloody cock, you're going to die!'
                    It wasn't long before
                    The fowl contracted worms,
And the dawn bugler had his gullet slit.
Did the girls' murder ease the terms
Of their employment? Quite the opposite.
                    Now, when they went to bed to rest,
                    They'd scarcely settled in it
Before the hag, fretting for each lost minute,
Went scolding round the house like one possessed.

That's how it often goes. Just when you're thinking
You're out of a nasty hole, you're sinking
                    Into the mud deeper.
The two girls got a worse deal – as time-keeper
An old witch in place of the old cock.
Tossed by the Whirlpool straight on to the Rock!

FABLE VII

THE SATYR AND THE TRAVELLER

In the depths of a primitive cave
A satyr and his foals
Were about to eat their broth,
Teeth champing the bowls.

Sire, dam and young ones stretched
On the moss made a pretty sight:
They had no carpet or cloth
But they had a good appetite.

Enter a traveller dodging
A cloudburst, chilled to the skin.
The unexpected guest
Was invited to come in.

His host hardly had time
To ask him twice to sup
Before he began to blow
On his fingers to warm them up;

This done, he gently puffed
On the food he was offered too.

The satyr was flabbergasted:
'Friend, what good does that do?'

'One breath for my broth to cool it,
And one for my hand to heat it.'
'Then be on your way again,'
Said the barbarous half-man. 'Beat it!

God save me from sharing a roof
With a creature like you. I don't hold
With someone who has a mouth
That can blow both hot and cold!'

FABLE IX

THE FARMER AND HIS SONS

Hard work, taking trouble –
There you have capital that's sure to double.

A rich farmer, feeling the onset of death,
Summoned his sons for a talk in private.
'Never,' he said with his remaining breath,
'Sell the heritage that is yours by birth
And was mine through my father and mother.
  Somewhere or other
A treasure lies hidden in that earth;
Where, I don't know, but in the end you'll arrive at
The right place, given some guts and toil.
When you've finished harvesting turn over your land,
Break it up, dig it, plough it, don't allow
One inch of it to escape your hand.'
The old man died, and the sons attacked the soil
So thoroughly with spade, mattock and plough
That at the year's end every field
  Gave them a bigger yield.
They never found that buried hoard;
And yet their father was no fool.
Before he died he taught the golden rule:
  Work is the hidden reward.

FABLE X

THE MOUNTAIN WHICH GAVE BIRTH

A mountain groaned so long and loud
In the pangs of labour that a crowd
Gathered, convinced that this, without a doubt,
    Was the moment of birth
    Of a new Paris on earth.
    Then a mouse crept out.

    This fable, which in one sense
    Is false but in another true,
    Puts me in mind of a poet I knew
    Who announced an immense
Forthcoming epic, *The Titans' War Against Zeus*.
    A great intention to declare –
But what do these vaunted pregnancies produce?
    Mostly hot air.

FABLE XII

THE DOCTORS

Dr It-can't-be-helped and Dr It-can
Met at the bedside of an ailing man.
The latter – though his colleague's grim prognosis
Was that the sufferer would soon be seeing
His ancestors – took a more hopeful view.
      Opinions disagreeing
As to medicaments and doses
And Dr It-can't-be-helped's having prevailed,
      Their patient failed
And paid mortality its due.

And so, considered either way,
Medical knowledge won the day.
'There,' said the first, 'he's dead –
Exactly as I prophesied!'
'If he'd trusted me,' the other replied,
'He'd still have years of life ahead.'

FABLE XIII

THE HEN WHO LAID GOLDEN EGGS

When greed attempts to win all, greed
Loses all. In support I only need
Cite the old story we've all heard
Of the man who owned a hen that used to lay
      A gold egg every day.
Convinced her gizzard was a treasure-vault,
He killed and opened up the bird,
Only to find an average specimen
      Of egg-producing hen.
      Thus he destroyed
      Through his own fault
The great bonanza he'd enjoyed.

For grabbers here's a pretty warning.
In recent years it's been a common sight
To see men ruined overnight
Who tried to make a fortune before morning.

FABLE XIV

THE DONKEY WHO WAS CARRYING HOLY RELICS

Carrying holy relics in a procession,
An ass imagined: 'All this homage belongs
To *me*, the incense and the songs
Are in *my* honour' – an impression
Which made him look ridiculously proud,
    Till someone in the crowd,
    Noticing his delusion, said:
'Dear Mr Donkey, you must rid your head
    Of this mad vanity.
It's the saint's image and not you
To whom the adoration's due:
The glory all belongs to Christianity.'

When magistrates are asses, we salute
The Law's regalia, not the dressed-up brute.

FABLE XVI

THE SNAKE AND THE FILE

The story goes that a snake, who lived next to a clock-maker
(It's bad luck when your neighbour's a house-breaker),
Entered his shop, looking for a meal,
And found nothing more palatable than a file made of steel,
  Which he proceeded to gnaw.
  The file, without getting angry, said:
'Poor ignorant animal, what are you trying to do?
  Little snake not right in the head,
  You're biting on more than you can chew.
  You won't get a farthing's worth of good cheer
  Out of me. Instead,
  You'll merely break your jaw.
  Time's are the only teeth I fear.'

This is addressed to you, spirits of the modern age,
Who, being talentless, are consumed by the serpent's gnashing rage.
  You torment yourselves in vain.
Do you think your barbarous fangs can make dents
In the myriad works of long-lived excellence?
  They remain,
  Unscarred,
  Brass-, steel-, diamond-hard.

FABLE XXI

THE DONKEY CLOTHED IN THE LION'S HIDE

When an ass dressed up in a lion's hide
Panic spread through the countryside;
Although an ass is far from brave
Everybody was terrified
    Until
The tip of an ear popped out and exposed the knave.
At once the punishment-stick
Did its job. People unwise
In the ways of mischief and cheating
Rubbed their astonished eyes
To see a donkey-boy beating
A cowed lion to the mill.

   Plenty of men in France
   Make a great song and dance
About their own importance. They are the folk
Who make this fable a familiar joke.
   Three-quarters of their bluster
Consists of the retinue their lords can muster.

FABLE VII

THE MULE WHO BOASTED OF HIS PEDIGREE

A bishop's mule, full of snobbish vainglory,
Talked incessantly of his mother, the mare –
    There was always some story
    Of how she'd done this or been there –
    And assumed that he deserved a place
    In the annals of his race
    Just for that. Later, when he became
A doctor's servant, he felt sick with shame.
In old age he was sent to the mill to grind.
Only then did his father, the ass, come back to his mind.

    Thus suffering can be a school
    To knock sense back into the fool,
    And men have every reason still
    To praise the good that comes from ill.

FABLE IX

THE STAG WHO SAW HIMSELF IN THE WATER

A stag, in the clear mirror of a stream,
Was considering his appearance. His self-esteem
Was gratified by his fine antlers, but his spindling
Shanks, whose image he saw dwindling
      Unimpressively away,
      Filled him with pained dismay.
Dolefully eyeing his reflection, he said:
'What disproportion between feet and head!
      My branched head overtops
      The branches of the highest copse,
      But my legs do me no credit.'
      Scarcely had he said it
Than a bloodhound appeared and forced him to make
A dash to the woods for safety's sake.
      There his antlers, those splendid
Ornaments, hindering every step, denied
The help his legs were eager to provide,
      Upon which his life depended.
Now he unsaid those words, regretting dearly
The gifts which Nature renewed on his brow yearly.

*

What is beautiful we prize;
What is merely useful we despise;
Yet what is beautiful is often our destruction.
The stag scorned the legs which lent him speed,
And cherished the horns which in his hour of need
Were a dire obstruction.

FABLE X

THE HARE AND THE TORTOISE

It's no good simply travelling fast;
What counts is not starting late –
As you'll see from the story I'm going to relate.
The tortoise once challenged the hare:
'Do you see that tree over there?
Let's have a race. I'll bet you come last.'
        'Last indeed!'
Retorted the animal famous for speed.
'Granny, take a dose of hellebore for your sanity's sake.'
'Sane or mad, I stand by my bet.'
'Done!' And by the tree each put down their stake.
What it was or who they agreed
To have as umpire isn't our affair.
        'Ready, get set . . . .'
There were only a few steps for our hare to take –
    I mean the sort of bounds
That a hare makes when, startled by hounds,
He sends them to the devil with a stride
That eats up miles of level countryside.
      Having, as I say, time to spare
      For napping, or for nibbling,

Or for sniffing out which way the wind was blowing,
He waited for the tortoise to get going.
Off she went, puffing and straining
Like an old senator, hobbling
As fast as she could, a pitiful rate.
        Meanwhile the hare,
Considering such a victory too cheap
And the prize hardly worth gaining,
Made it a point of honour to start late.
        He had a little feed,
        And then a little sleep,
He thought of everything but the race to be run.
Then he saw the tortoise almost at the winning-post
And was off like a flash at last, with a giant leap.
        Too late! The tortoise had won.
'Well!' she exclaimed. 'Didn't I make good my boast?
        What use is all your speed?
        Absolutely none!
How much farther behind do you think you'd be
If you had a house to carry like me!'

FABLE XIII

THE PEASANT AND THE SNAKE

Aesop tells of a peasant with a kind
Heart but a rather simple mind
Who on a winter's day going the round
Of his acres noticed on the snowy ground
An adder numbed with cold, stiff as a board,
Bound in a matter of minutes to expire.
He picked the snake up and, returning
Home, with no thought of earning
Thanks for his good deed laid it by the fire.
Slowly the paralysed body thawed
Till life, with heat, came back to the creature,
And with new life its angry reptile nature.
At first it feebly reared its head and hissed,
Then coiled its length and tried to strike, but missed,
Its benefactor, foster-father, saviour.
'Ungrateful thing!' he cried. 'Is this my reward?
Die, then, for your behaviour!'
And in a righteous fury seized his axe
And with two mighty hacks
Made of the tail, the middle and the head
Three little snakes, all dead.

They writhed and squirmed to join themselves again,
But writhed and squirmed in vain.

It's a fine thing to be kind, but it all depends:
Kind to whom? As for ingrates who turn on friends,
Sooner or later they come to sticky ends.

FABLE XVI

THE HORSE AND THE DONKEY

In this world we must help each other. Why?
Because if your neighbour happens to die
It's on you that the burden will fall.

An ass was travelling with a coarse
And unobliging horse,
The latter carrying no weight at all
But his harness, while the poor ass was weighed down
So cruelly he was staggering on the road.
He begged the horse to shoulder part of his load.
'My request is not unreasonable,' he said.
'For you half of my load would be child's play.'
The horse retorted 'Nay!'
And added a loud fart.
After the donkey had dropped dead
The horse saw his error; for in the end
He was made to pull a cart
With the same load plus the carcass of his friend.

FABLE XVII

THE DOG WHO DROPPED THE SUBSTANCE
FOR THE SHADOW

Everyone under the sun
Deceives himself: so many madmen run
After shadows that one's half the time unable
To reckon their number up.
We must refer them to the fable
In which Aesop speaks of the foolish pup.

This young dog, carrying a dead rabbit
And seeing its reflection in a stream,
Opened his jaws, tried to grab it,
And was almost drowned
When the river suddenly turned choppy.
He just managed to regain dry ground –
Without either substance or dream,
Original or copy.

FABLE III

THE RAT WHO RETIRED FROM THE WORLD

Here's an old story the Levantines tell.
A rat, weary of the troubles of this world,
Retired into a Dutch cheese. Profound
Was the global silence stretching all around
      Our new hermit curled,
        Far from care, in his nourishing cell.
    Within days his teeth and feet
Had gnawed and dug so deep that his retreat
Offered not merely board but bed as well.
What more was there to do? He grew sleek and fat –
      For God most generously endows
      Those who take other-worldly vows.
      One day our devout rat
      Was visited by a deputation
Of rats on their way abroad in search of aid
      Towards raising the blockade
      Of Ratopolis by the cat nation.
Due to the poverty of their hard-pressed city
They'd had to leave with nothing in the kitty
For travelling expenses. 'A small sum
Is all we ask. Fellow-citizen, take pity!
In a week at the most rescue is sure to come.'
      'Friends,' said the anchorite,

'I no longer concern myself with this world's affairs.
    How can a poor recluse
    Be of any use
To you here, except by offering up prayers?
Heaven help you in your plight!
May God grant you His merciful grace!'
So saying, he shut the door in their face.

Whom do you think I'm pointing at
In the figure of the ungenerous rat?
    A Christian father?
    A heathen dervish rather!
For monks unfailingly relieve
Distress – at least so I believe.

VI

FABLE IV

THE HERON

One day the heron was out walking –
Don't ask me where, just stalking
On his long legs, with his long neck and beak,
      Up some creek
      Whose water was as clear
As on the brightest morning of the year.
      There granny carp
Was weaving circles with her crony pike.
It would have been easy for the heron to strike –
They were there for the taking, right by the verge –
But he thought it better to restrain his urge
      Until his appetite got sharp
(He was eating at set times, on a strict regime).
After a bit his appetite returned
      And, going closer, he discerned
Tench swimming up from their haunts in the stream.
      Thinking: 'What scruffy fish!
      I can do better than that,'
      For he was as hard to satisfy
      As Horace's town rat,
'Tench!' he exclaimed. 'What should I,
The heron, have to do with such small fry?
Who do you take me for?' Having scorned that dish,

He noticed some gudgeon. 'Gudgeon!'
          He said to himself in dudgeon.
'That's no lunch for a heron. Heaven forbid
I should open my beak for mere tiddlers. Ugh!'
          But open his beak he did
All day, for less and less, while the fish hid,
Till his hunger-pangs got so bad
          He was positively glad
          To come across a slug.

Don't be too dainty about choosing:
The most adaptable men are the most clever;
If you want too much you may end up losing.
          Never
          Be over-nicely grand,
Especially when you've nearly enough in hand.

FABLE VII

THE LION'S COURT

His Majesty the lion, having a mind
      To ascertain
How many nations Heaven had assigned
      To his domain,
Sent couriers north, east, south and west
To all his subjects of the animal kind
With a circular letter, personally signed.
      The document's import
      Was that the royal beast
For the next month would hold open court,
The programme starting with a sumptuous feast
Followed by clowns and jugglers and such sport.
      This generous act
      Was a parade of power in fact.
He asked them to his palace. Palace? A place
More like a charnel-house, whose stench attacked
The nostrils of his guests! The bear
Stopped his nose. He should have dispensed
      With that grimace;
It didn't please the monarch, who, incensed,
Sent him to Hades to be squeamish there.
      The monkey broke into applause
At this harsh treatment. Being a toadying slave,

He praised the king's anger, the king's claws,
       Even the royal cave,
Whose smell, he swore, was exquisite –
Roses or ambergris compared with it
Were garlic. His gross flattery did not
Succeed: he paid the penalty on the spot
(For this almighty lion was as evil
As Rome's Caligula). The fox, poor devil,
Was standing by. 'Well, sirrah,' said the king,
       'What do *you* smell?
       Speak without paltering!'
       The fox, hunting for a way out,
Pleaded a bad cold: 'With my suffering snout
       I can hardly tell
One scent from another.' He escaped well.

This story has a lesson to teach.
At court, if you desire to please,
       Avoid trite flatteries,
       Never employ blunt speech,
And on the odd occasion try
The Norman trick, a devious reply.

FABLE IX

THE COACH AND THE FLY

Up a steep, sandy, difficult road
Exposed on all sides to the sun's heat
Six strong coach-horses were pulling their load,
Labouring, sweating, out of breath, dead-beat
(The passengers had taken to their feet),
When a fly arrived and, circling round the team,
    Attempted with her puny scream
     To urge them on, planting her sting
On flank and buttock, perching on the pole,
Even on the driver's nose, imagining
    All the time that it was owing
To her efforts that the coach kept going.
Each time the wheels managed to roll
And the travellers walked some yards of ground,
Assuming that the credit must all go
To her, she fussed pompously to and fro
    Like a colonel dashing around
    Shouting 'Forwards!' on the field,
Frantic to force the enemy to yield.
In this shared emergency Mrs Fly
    Was full of reproach:

'Who's helping the horses pull the coach?
Who's taking responsibility? Only I.
The monk's been saying his prayers –
What a fine time for spiritual affairs!
   One woman was singing a song –
As if that would move the coach along!'
In every ear she buzzed and whirred,
Her words and actions equally absurd.
With a great deal more work the team climbed the grade.
At once the fly announced: 'Let's stop
   For a breather here in the shade.
All our passengers have reached the top
   Entirely thanks to me.
Now then, horses, what about my fee?'

Some people fuss and meddle and advise.
Though they seem to be doing what needs to be done,
They're a damned nuisance to everyone
And should be chased away like flies.

FABLE X

THE DAIRYMAID AND THE MILK-CAN

With a milk-can on her head
Set firmly on a pad,
Here comes Perrette,
Hoping to walk to town without an upset.
Short-skirted and lightly clad,
She strides along with a quick tread,
Having today, for greater ease,
Put on flat-heeled shoes and a plain chemise.
Already our dairymaid
Is lost in a waking dream
Of all the money she's going to be paid
For the milk she'll sell at the fair,
And afterwards how she'll spend it there:
She'll buy a hundred eggs and breed
Three times as many chicks. With work and care,
She tells herself, the scheme
Is certain to succeed.
'It won't be very hard
To raise the chicks in my back-yard;
The fox will have to be extra stealthy
Not to leave me enough to purchase a pig,
To fatten the pig won't cost me much in feed
(I must have bought him reasonably big),

And when I sell him I'll be really wealthy!
Then, with the proceeds, what's to stop
Me fitting up our stable for a cow,
And her calf too? I can see it now
       In my mind's eye
Skipping and frisking with the herd. . . .'
      Here, suiting deed to word,
      Perrette gave a rapturous hop –
      And lost her balance and her load.
Chickens and pig and cow and calf, goodbye!
      Her fortune spilt on the road,
      The owner of all that stock
      With a woebegone expression
Went home to her husband to make her confession.
      I expect he gave her a knock.
So ends my farcical recital,
Which has 'The Milk-can' for a title.

Who doesn't build castles in Spain?
Which of us isn't mildly insane?
Picrochole, Pyrrhus, the dairymaid,
Wise men and fools alike, we all daydream
      (No pleasure in life is so sweet)
      And each of us is betrayed
      By flattering self-deceit –
The world's riches and honours seem
Ours then, and all its lovely women at our feet.
      Whenever I'm alone
My imagination rambles, I browbeat
Heroes, topple the great Shah from his throne,
The adoring populace hail me instead
And diadems are showered on my head –
Until some little mishap ends my reign
      And I'm my old fat self again.

FABLE XI

THE PRIEST AND THE CORPSE

A corpse was mournfully being trundled
      To its last resting-place,
      Escorted on its way
      By a curé with a cheerful face
Eager to bury it without delay.
The late deceased, all neatly bundled,
      Lay in that robe of lead
We call a coffin – clothes the luckless dead
      Can never change, no matter
How hot or cold the season of the year.
      The priest beside the bier
Was running through his routine patter
Of hymns and psalms and exhortations
And prayers and scriptural quotations.
'My dear dead friend, leave it to me,'
He seemed to say, 'I'll bury you in style –
      Providing I receive my fee.'
Here he devoured the coffin with his eyes
As though he might be cheated of his prize,
His looks declaring all the while:
'My dear dead friend, I'm going to screw
      A sum of money out of you

Plus so many candles, not to mention
Several extra sundries too.'
By now he saw himself as having paid
    For a sizeable flagon
Of the best local wine and a new smock
For his pretty niece and his chambermaid.
    This pleasurable intention
Was interrupted by the shock
Of an accident. From the funeral wagon
The dead man in his box of lead
Came crashing on his curé's head,
And so parishioner and pastor
Went hand in hand to meet their Master.

    Eyes fixed on the distance,
    Counting on more than they'll get,
    How typical of our existence
Are the curé and the dairymaid Perrette!

FABLE XIII

THE TWO COCKS

Two cocks were living in peace. A certain hen
      Came on the scene – and then
      War burst into flame.
O Love, you ruined Troy, you were to blame
For that envenomed quarrel which once stained
The river Xanthus with the gods' own blood!
For a long time these cocks maintained
A running battle, while the neighbourhood
Rang with the racket of their fight
And the crested tribe ran up to watch the sight;
      For the winner would enjoy
A bevy of fine-feathered Helens of Troy.
The loser fled and, cowering in his coop,
Bewailed his lost prestige and, worse, the wives
      His rival, cock-a-hoop,
      Possessed before his very eyes.
But soon this daily spectacle revives
His hate, his nerve. He whets his beak,
He flaps his wings and beats his sides, he trains,
Sparring with shadows, till his jealous pique
      Has made him battle-proof.
He needn't have taken all those pains;
For his conqueror, now perching on a roof

And crowing his song of victory, was heard
        By quite another sort of bird.
Farewell, glory! Farewell, feathered Helens!
His pride was shredded by a vulture's talons.
            Thus, in the end, by one of luck's
            Cruel turns his rival for the hen
            Became cock-of-the-walk again,
            Surrounded by his *poules de luxe*.
I leave you to imagine all the clucks. . . .

Fate loves to stage a plot with twists:
The insolent conqueror assists
In his own downfall. Let us despise
Fortune by all means; let us too be wise
In victory to guard against surprise.

FABLE XVI

THE CAT, THE WEASEL AND THE YOUNG RABBIT

One fine day
The house of a young rabbit was taken over
By her ladyship the weasel – a low, weasely
Trick, for the master having gone away
To pay the Dawn his court
Among the dewy thyme and clover,
She got in easily
With all her household goods, and squatted.
After he'd nibbled and trotted
And scampered and enjoyed his sport,
Returning again
To his lodgings underground
John Rabbit found
The intruder there, snout pressed against the pane.
Barred from the home his parents used to inhabit,
'By all the gods of hospitality
What on earth's this?' exclaimed the rabbit.
'Why, it's Lady Weasel. Well, you'd better get out
At once, without a fuss, or else I'll shout
For all the rats in the locality!'
The sharp-nosed lady snapped back: 'Land or lair
Belongs to the occupant who's *there*.
Anyway what a subject for a squabble –
A hole one has to crawl into bent double!
If this were a kingdom I should like to know

What statute you could cite
That guarantees the right
Of ownership in perpetuity
To John, nephew or son of Bill or Joe,
Rather than Tom – or for that matter me.'
John Rabbit pleaded in his cause
Tradition, custom. 'Those are the laws,'
He argued, 'that assign
The lordship of this house to me and mine,
By which the property's been handed on
Through grandfather and father to me, John –
Laws twice as valid as your "squatter's right".'
'So what? Enough of all this talking,
Let's take our case to the great Grimalkin.'
(This was a cat who lived like an anchorite,
A Jesuitical,
Hypocritical,
Smily,
Purry,
Wily,
Furry,
Sleek and fat
Lawyer of a cat,
Long versed in the arts of arbitrating.)
Rabbit agreed. Soon both were waiting
On the front-door mat
Of his ermine-furred
Worship. 'Come in, come in,' he purred,
'Please move much closer, my dears,
For I'm rather deaf with my advancing years.'
Seeing no cause to be afraid,
The litigants obeyed.
Once they were in his reach old Santa Claws
Shot out two simultaneous paws

And to his satisfaction
Settled the action
By crunching them impartially in his jaws.

This is the sort of thing
That happens when inferior princes bring
Their quarrels to the judgement of a king.

VII

FABLE XVII

THE HEAD AND THE TAIL OF THE SNAKE

The snake has a head in front and a tail behind;
      Both are enemies of mankind
And among the cruel Fates have great repute.
      Long ago this led
      To a serious dispute
Over the right of precedence. The head
      Having invariably been
      The leader until then, the tail
Addressed to Heaven an indignant wail.
'At her caprice I'm dragged for miles,' she said.
'Does she think I'll stand for being humiliated
For ever? I thank God that He created
Us sisters, not attendant slave and queen.
      Since both of us once came
From the same mother, treat us both the same:
My sting's as sharp as hers and kills as soon.
      This, then, is the boon
      I crave. You must ordain
That from now on our roles will be reversed:
The head shall be last and the tail shall be first,
      And I'll be such a trusty guide
That nobody can be dissatisfied.'
Heaven heard her and was cruelly kind:

When God assents it often causes pain;
He should be deaf to prayers when they are blind.
He wasn't this time, though. The new path-finder,
    Who in broad day could see no more
Than if she'd been inside an oven door,
After colliding with a marble chunk,
      A passer-by and a tree-trunk
      Led her sister behind her
      Straight into the Stygian lake.

Ill-starred the state that makes the same mistake!

FABLE II

THE COBBLER AND THE BUSINESSMAN

There was a cobbler who sang all day long;
It would have made your heart rejoice
To see him at it or to hear a song.
He trilled, he warbled – what a marvellous voice!
   What's more, he lived at peace
With his own soul, like the seven wise men of Greece.
His neighbour, on the other hand, a man
Rolling in money, hardly sang at all
And slept even less. Often, when dawn had broken
And he was lightly dozing, he'd be woken
By the cobbler carolling and fretfully think:
   'Why didn't Providence plan
Things better so that sleep, like food or drink,
Was purchasable at any market-stall?'
One day he asked the singer round to visit
His grand house. 'Now tell me how much money
You make in a year, Mr Gregory – what is it?'
'In a year? God bless us, sir,' the other said
As if he found the question rather funny,

   'It's not my habit to count
The pennies up, I wouldn't know the amount;
I live from day to day; I'm quite content
If at the year's end I'm not overspent.
   Each day brings in its bread.'

'Well, then, what do you make daily?'
'Sometimes more, sometimes less,' the cobbler answered gaily.
    'The worst of it is, they've made
So many days of the year into holidays,
    And on them we're forced to laze.
But for that we'd do all right; as it is, our trade
Is being ruined, for one Church feast
Cuts the throat of another and each week our priest
Saddles his sermon with some brand-new saint.'
    'How naive, how quaint!'
    Thought the millionaire.
'Today,' he announced, 'I propose to give you a throne.
Here are a hundred crowns – they're now your own.
Guard them against a rainy day with care.'
In the cobbler's eyes they looked like centuries' worth
Of precious metal yielded by the earth
    For the convenience of mankind.
He hurried home and underneath the floor
Buried his money – and his peace of mind.
    From that day on he sang no more:
    The moment he laid hands upon
The source of human sorrow his voice was gone.
    Sleep deserted his bed,
And in his home he entertained instead
Groundless suspicions and wild fears.
All day he strained his eyes and ears,
And if at night a stray cat made a board
Creak, he imagined thieves were at his hoard.
    In the end the poor chap ran
    Back to the house of the businessman
(By now no longer an insomniac)
    And shouted: 'There, you keep
    Your hundred crowns and give me back
    My songs and my lost sleep!'

FABLE V

THE MAN AND THE FLEA

With our importunate prayers we tire heaven,
Often for favours that are unworthy even
Of men to beg. As if, forgoing sleep,
  The gods are obliged to keep
Watch over all us mannikins day and night
And the least mere mortal has a right,
   At every turn,
   Each step forward he makes,
   Each petty plan he undertakes,
   To bother Olympus and to bore
The gods and goddesses with his concern
As though the subject were the Trojan war!

A fool, bitten in the shoulder by a flea
Which had lodged in the folds of his toga,
  At once called on Hercules:
'It's up to you, when spring comes round, to free
The world of this troublesome ogre.
And what are you doing on your cloudy height,
Jupiter? Why don't you avenge my bite
  By blasting the whole race of fleas?'

To crush one bug he thought he could invoke
The hero's club and Jove's own lightning-stroke!

FABLE VI

WOMEN AND SECRETS

A secret is the heaviest load:
To carry one even a few steps down the road
Is hard for a woman; and many men – I speak
With experience – are femininely weak.

One night a husband, to test his bride
Beside him in the darkness, suddenly cried:
'Good God! What's happening? I can't bear it! My flesh
Is being torn apart! Merciful heaven,
  I'm giving . . . aaah, I've given
  Birth to an egg!' 'An egg?'
  'Yes, there it is, right by my leg,
  Absolutely fresh.
But don't tell anyone, in fact not a single word,
Or people will go round calling me a bird.'
  Knowing little of life
And still less of a case like this, the young wife
  Believed it and solemnly swore
To keep her lips sealed, then and for evermore.
  But with the shadows of the night
  That promise faded away.
Being indiscreet and not too bright,

She jumps out of bed at the peep of day
And runs round to her neighbour:
'Mother, the strangest thing has just occurred –
    But please don't breathe a word
    Or you'll get me a beating.
Last night my husband went into labour
And produced an egg as big as *that*.
This is a secret strictly not for repeating,
In God's name keep it under your hat.'
'Don't be silly,' says the other. 'Ah, my dear,
You don't know me. Go home. Have no fear.'
While the egg-layer's wife was returning,
The old biddy, of course, was burning
To be the first with the news. Off she races
And spreads it in a dozen different places.
    Her version adds two eggs more.
    Worse follows: another crone
    Whispers in someone's ear – an act
By now of supernumerary discretion –
    That she knows for a fact
    That the number was four.
From mouth to mouth, by rumorous progression,
By the end of the day the total has grown
    To well above five score.

FABLE VIII

THE JOKER AND THE FISH

Others say jokers are the salt of the earth;
    I give them a wide berth.
Above all other arts, the humourist's needs
      Supreme touch.
God made the wretched wag and his wit
      Solely for fools' benefit.
I shall now venture to introduce one such
      Into a fable,
        Which he who reads
May perhaps be kind enough to think succeeds.

A humourist dining at a magnate's table,
Finding at his end only titchy fish
(All the big ones were on a far dish),
      Picked up his small fry,
Put his mouth to their ears, spoke
A few words, and completed his fishy joke
By making as if to listen to their reply.
      Amazement on all sides;
Good cheer, interrupted, subsides.
Then the man announces in a sober tone

That he fears that a friend of his, India-bound
        A year ago,
May have been shipwrecked and drowned,
And proceeds to ask for news from his handful of sprats.
With one voice (his) they reply: 'We're not fully enough grown
To be sure what happened to him. That's
        Something big fish would know.'
'Then, gentlemen, may I ask a turbot about my friend?'
        Whether his jest
        Appealed to the rest
Of the company I doubt; but in the end
He induced them to put on his plate
A monster of a fish, ancient enough to relate
The names of all the adventurers who'd explored
        New worlds and been lost on board –
Bones going back a century,
Bones of the deep that could only be
Familiar to the veterans of the vasty sea.

FABLE X

THE BEAR AND THE GARDEN-LOVER

A certain half-licked mountain bear
Confined by Fate to the remotest lair
    Of the woods, living at odds
With the world (just like Bellerophon,
The hero hated by the gods),
Was going mad; for it's well known
That creatures soon do when they're left alone.
        Talk is good,
Silence is better still, but both are bad
When people carry them too far.
No beast set foot in that wild neighbourhood,
So that at last (bears being what they are)
He became sick of his miserable existence.
While he was busy being sad,
All this time an old eccentric loner
Was living within walking distance
    And feeling just as bored.
He was a garden-lover who adored
The goddess Flora, and likewise Pomona.
It's all right cultivating fruit and flowers,
    But in between I'd recommend

The presence of a sober, sensitive friend.
Gardens don't talk, except in poetry books!
    And so, tired of long hours
Among his flower-folk with their speechless looks,
One fine morning he set off to find
Some company in the countryside.
At the same time, with the same thing in mind,
    The bear began to descend
From his mountain home, and by a freak of chance
The two met, coming round a bend.
    The man was terrified.
What should he do? Retreat? Stand still? Advance?
Since the best thing in such a case
Is to put on a brazen Gascon face,
He managed to disguise his fright.
The bear, not used to being polite,
Growled: 'Visit my lair.' The other replied.
'Noble sir, you can see my cottage.
Will you do me the honour of eating there?
It's a rustic meal – fruit, milk and pottage –
    Probably not the regular fare
    Of a most distinguished bear,
    But what I have is yours to share.'
    The bear consented.
On the way they soon became a cordial pair;
Once they arrived the friendship was cemented,
    For though as a general rule
It's better to live alone than with a fool,
Since most of the day his guest remained quite mute
The man was free to tend his flowers and fruit.
    Meanwhile the simple brute
Went off hunting and brought back game
Or else indulged his favourite pursuit
Of catching insects; often he would keep

Those wingéd pests ('flies' is the vulgar name)
From his friend's face when he dropped off to sleep.
One day a fly perched on the nose of the man
When he was sunk in dreams and drove the bear
For all his vaunted prowess to despair.
'I'll get you this time!' Done as soon as said.
The faithful swatter carried out his plan.
Hurling a paving-stone as hard as he could,
He crushed the fly – and with it his host's head.
Marksmanship excellent; thinking not so good,
Where a man had been, a corpse was stretched instead.

An enemy with common sense
Is far less dangerous than a friend who's dense.

FABLE XI

THE TWO FRIENDS

Two bosom friends once lived in Hyderabad,
Sharing in common everything they had.
(I've heard that friendships are at least
As strong as ours are in the East.)

One night when both were busy sleeping,
Profiting from the absence of the sun,
One of them woke in alarm and, leaping
Out of his bed, ran to the house of the other
And roused his servants – for by now the Lord
    Of Slumber had set foot
Within the palace gates. The sleeping one,
Startled, reached for his purse and sword
And left his room to meet his brother.
    'It's a rare thing for you,' he said,
'To be abroad when all the world's in bed:
You've always struck me as a man who'd put
To better use the sacred hours of night.
Have you lost a fortune gambling? Well, if so,
Here's money. Have you got into a fight?
    I've brought my sword – let's go!
    Are you tired of lying in the dark

Night after night on your own?
I've just come from beside
A pretty concubine. She's yours on loan –
Shall I call her over?' 'No,' his friend replied.
          'You haven't hit the mark.
But thank you for your kind zeal all the same.
          The truth is that I dreamed
          A dream in which you seemed
          Unhappy, so I came
          Rushing across, fearing the worst.
          It was my accursed
Nightmare that was to blame.'

Which of these two was the fonder?
There's a good question to ponder.
What do you think, reader, I wonder?
          A true friend is a pearl. He reads
          Your deepest needs
          And so spares you the shame
Of giving your heart's hidden desires a name.
          When somebody is very dear,
A dream, anything, nothing stirs your fear.

FABLE XV

THE RAT AND THE ELEPHANT

Having ideas above one's station
Is very common in France. One often sees
A man behaving with a lordly air
Who's actually a tradesman or a mayor.
It's a typically French disease,
This stupid vanity, peculiar to our nation.
Spaniards are vain, but not in the same way.
Their pride strikes me as, in a word,
Far crazier but less absurd.
Let me give you an illustration:
It will do as well as another to point what I have to say.

An exceptionally small rat,
Seeing an elephant who was exceptionally fat,
      Scoffed
        At the somewhat leisurely pace
Of that beast of honourable and ancient race,
Who was carrying massive tackle aloft.
      A sultan in all his glory,
      Pilgrimage-bound, in a three-storey
      Howdah, was *en voyage*, complete
With household slaves, sultana, parakeet,

Pet monkey, dog and cat.
The rat thought it amazing
That an awed crowd should be gazing
At that ponderous bulk. 'As if,' fumed Rat,
'The respect that each of us is worth
Depends on how much space we occupy on earth!
What do you people see in him to marvel at?
Is this the great bogey that makes children scream?
Small though we are, we rats esteem
Ourselves as every bit
As good as elephants.' He was warming to his theme,
But the cat, bounding from his wicker frame,
In less time than it takes to say 'knife'
Made him run for his life,
Ready to admit
That elephants and rats are not the same.

FABLE XXIII

THE TORRENT AND THE RIVER

With a thunderous roar of foam
A cataract hurtled from its mountain home.
Everything fled before it; in its wake
Horror followed; it made the neighbourhood quake.
No traveller had dared to try to force
A passage through its furious course,
  Till a solitary stranger,
Seeing a robber band and spurred by danger,
Put the torrent between them and his horse
By fording the fierce water – which in fact
For all its raging wasn't very deep.
    And so our man got clear
With nothing worse than the dry taste of fear.
Heartened by this, but still being tracked
By the same brigands, further on he met
A river which seemed the image of sweet sleep,
Tranquil and halcyon, the banks not steep,
The sand so clean and bright he was sure he'd get
Easily across. His horse, this second time,
Rescued him from the robbers dogging him,
  But not from the black slime.
Both man and beast were dragged below

To drink the Styx and joylessly to swim
    As shadows to and fro
In rivers quite unlike the ones we know.

Beware of people who are quiet and calm:
The noisy ones won't do you any harm.

FABLE XXVI

DEMOCRITUS AND THE ABDERITES

How I've always hated the view of the multitude,
Which seems to me prejudiced, hasty, crude
      And alien to God,
Interposing between itself and things a distorting lens
      And measuring other men's
      Stature by its own small rod.
      This universal feature
Was experienced by Epicurus' teacher
Whose countrymen thought he was out of his mind.
      Pitiful fools! But there you are –
      No man is a prophet among his own kind.
It was they who were mad, Democritus was wise.
      The people's delusion went so far
      That his native city sent overseas
      Letters and envoys to the famous
      Physician Hippocrates
To come and restore the wits of the lunatic.
'Our fellow-citizen,' they said with tears in their eyes,
'Has gone mad: too much reading has made him sick.

We should honour him more if he were an ignoramus.
   Why, he avers
That there are innumerable worlds, even that all of them contain
   Identical philosophers
   Named Democritus! Not contented
   With this notion, he has invented
Invisible ghosts called atoms, creatures of his crazed brain;
   And now he sits
Motionless on the earth, measuring heaven's dimensions,
Wandering in space – and in his wits.
Once he knew how to reconcile our dissensions,
   But these days he'll only speak
   To himself. Help us, godlike Greek,
   For his folly has reached new heights.'
Although he hadn't much faith in the Abderites,
The doctor went with them. Now observe, please,
   What strange coincidences
Chance produces in life. Hippocrates
   Happened to arrive during the week
When the man who was said to have lost his senses
Was attempting to establish in which part
Of the body, among animals and men,
The intelligence is seated, whether head or heart.
   Picture him, then,
Sitting under a thick-leaved tree, beside a brook,
Engrossed in the convolutions of a skull.
   With many a learned book
Piled at his feet and his mind, as usual, full,
He almost failed to notice his old friend coming.
Civilities were brief, as you'd expect:
The wise are sparing with both time and speech.
Dispensing with small talk, they fell to plumbing
   The nature of Man, his soul and intellect,
   And then embarked on ethics. There's no need

For me to divulge or you to read
The various arguments advanced by each.

   The foregoing example
   Furnishes us with ample
Evidence to impugn the judgement of the many.
   Can that tag which I recall
Reading somewhere, ever be true, in any
   Context at all?
   May I
Remind you: '*Vox populi, vox Dei.*'

FABLE IV

THE ACORN AND THE PUMPKIN

Whatever God does, He does for the best.
No need to scour the world from east to west
For proof of that: I find it in a pumpkin.

    A country bumpkin,
    Considering this fruit, its huge girth
And thin stalk, exclaimed: 'What on earth
Was the Creator thinking of, putting the pumpkin there?
    Upon my word, I swear
    That if it had been up to me
    I'd have hung it on a tree –
An oak, that's it, would have been the very one to suit
    So tremendous a fruit!
A pity, my lad, you've never been able to figure
The ways of God that our priest teaches in church;
If you had, you wouldn't be needing to search
    For explanations. Take the case
    Of the acorn: it's no bigger
Than my little finger – why not hang it in the pumpkin's place?
    The longer I ponder
    On this mix-up, the more I wonder

How He came to make such an almighty blunder.'
　　This puzzle bothered the simple hind.
'When a man's been blessed with a lively mind
　　He gets no sleep,' he sighed, and soon
Went off to take a nap under an oak.
An acorn fell hard on the sleeper's nose; he awoke
And, clapping a hand to his face, found the thing stuck
　　In his beard. His bruised nose
　　Made our philosopher change his tune:
'Ouch! It's bleeding! All the same, what luck
For me it was nothing heavier. Just suppose
　　The acorn had been a gourd!
　　But that was not the way the Lord
　　Wanted it. He was perfectly right –
　　And now I can see why.'
　　The man went home that night
Praising God for all things under the sky.

FABLE IX

THE OYSTER AND THE LITIGANTS

One day two travellers, walking side by side,
Came on an oyster washed up by the tide.
Greedily they devoured it with their eyes,
Excitedly they pointed out its size,
And then, inevitably, they faced
The problem: which of them as judge
Should pass a verdict on the taste?
One was already stooping for the prize
When his friend gave him a nudge:
    'We must decide this properly.
    The epicure's monopoly
Belongs to whoever saw it first: *he* swallows
The oyster and, it logically follows,
    The other has to watch him do it.'
    'If that's the way you view it,
I have, thank God, remarkably keen sight.'
    'Mine's pretty good as well,
    And upon my life I swear
I saw it before you!' 'So what? All right,
    You may have been

The first to *see*, but I was the first to *smell*.'
Who should arrive upon this charming scene
But Perrin Dandin? Asked to intervene
  As arbiter in the affair,
  With a portentous air
  He digs the oyster from its shell
And gulps it while his audience stands and stares.
  The meal finished, he declares
In the tone of voice beloved of presidents:
  'The court hereby decrees
An award, without costs, of one shell to each.
  Both parties please
  Proceed without a breach
Of the peace to your lawful residence.'

Count what it costs these days to go to court,
And how little the families driven to that resort
Have left after expenses. It's the Law,
It's Perrin Dandin who eats up the rest –
  Who takes the wing and breast
And leaves the litigants the beak and claw.

FABLE XVI

THE HIDDEN TREASURE AND THE TWO MEN

A bankrupt, an unrescuable debtor
    With the devil lodged in his poke
    (In other words, dead broke),
    Reckoned he could do no better
    Than hang himself and be done
With his miserable life, since in the long run
Hunger, without his help, was sure to end it –
A way of death with little to commend it
To those who have no appetite for dying.
    The would-be suicide
Chose as the stage on which to 'end it all'
A ruined cottage. He brought cord for tying
The noose, a hammer and a nail, then tried
To fix a halter high up on one wall.
    The wall, being very frail and old,
Collapsed at the first blow – and revealed a hoard of gold.
Our desperate hero, leaving the rope behind,
Collected and took home the whole amount,
    Which he didn't even count:
    Thereabouts or all told,
    What did he care?

He was more than satisfied.
While he was departing with a jaunty stride,
The owner of the treasure arrived to find
                Nothing there.
        'Dear God, I would rather have died
        Than lose that money,' he cried,
'I would rather have hanged myself. . . . In fact I might,
        If only there were a rope in sight.'
        The noose was at hand, it only lacked
The man to knot it and perform the act.
He did it perfectly. I like to hope
                He was consoled
By the thought that someone else had paid for the rope.
So the cord found a new master as well as the gold.

Misers usually end their days in grief;
They get the least share of their hoarded treasure,
        Losing it in the end to a thief,
To relatives or simply to the earth.
But what should we make of Fortune's strange
Practical joke? That's how she is; we are her source of mirth:
The odder the twist, the greater her pleasure.
        The goddess who loves change
        Took it into her head
To watch a man hang himself; and he who erected
His own gallows was the one who least expected
                To end up dead.

FABLE III

THE TORTOISE AND THE TWO DUCKS

A simple-minded tortoise,
        Tired of living curled
In her hole, conceived a desire to see the world.
It's easy to glamorize foreign places;
Lame folk get to hate their own cramped quarters.
        Two ducks, to whom the dear old Gran
Confided her ambition, at once proposed a plan
To help her: 'Do you see that great route up there?
We'll take you along it to America, by air.
You'll see all sorts of kingdoms, republics, races;
The different customs you'll observe will broaden your mind.
        Why, Ulysses did the same.'
Although she'd hardly expected the hero's name
        To be introduced here,
        The tortoise liked the idea
And a deal was made. Soon the birds had designed
A machine by which the voyager could ascend.
        Jamming a stick in her mouth crosswise
        And telling her: 'Bite hard! Don't let go!'
        Each of them gripped it at one end.
Up went the tortoise, and the world rubbed its eyes

To see the proverbially slow,
House-bound creature soaring with a duck on either side.
'A miracle!' somebody cried.
'Come and look at the queen of the tortoises sailing the skies!'
'The queen! Why, yes, that's exactly who I am –
And don't let anyone scoff!'
She would have been far better off
To have made her flight in silence like a clam,
For, unclenching her teeth,
She dropped the stick, fell and was smashed to bits at the feet
Of the gazers beneath,
Her folly the cause of her death.

Garrulousness, inanity,
Inquisitiveness and vanity,
All spring from one parent seed,
Are all children of the same narrow breed.

FABLE XIII

THE LIONESS AND THE BEAR

A hunter having trapped and taken
    Her cub, the lioness
Gave vent to such wild roarings of distress
That the whole forest was disturbed and shaken.
    Neither Night's darkness nor her peace
    Nor any of her secret joys
    Could make the great beast cease
    From her intolerable noise –
No other animal could sleep a wink.
At last the bear spoke up: 'Madam, just think
How many of our young – cub, calf or kid –
Have died for your carnivorous diet.
Didn't *they* have parents?' 'Yes, they did.'
    'Then if that's true
And if the deaths the rest of us have had
To endure have failed to drive *us* mad,
If the other mourning mothers have kept quiet,
Why can't you suffer in silence too?'
'Suffer in silence? Me? In my state?
I've lost my child! Joyless old age awaits me!'
'What power condemns you to this miserable fate?'
'Poor me! It must be Destiny who hates me!'

'Madam, since the first mother lost a son
Those words have passed the lips of everyone.'

This is addressed to you, weak human race.
I hear nothing but trivial complaints!
    If anyone in a similar case
Imagines that God hates him above all men,
Let him remember Hecuba – and then
    Give thanks to all the saints.

FABLE VIII

THE OLD MAN AND THE THREE YOUTHS

An octogenarian was on his knees
    Engaged in planting trees.
'To build a house makes sense, but to embark
On planting at that age is downright odd:
He must be losing his grip,' was the remark
Made by three youths watching him, sons of neighbours.
    'Sir, in the name of God,'
One of them asked, 'how can an old boy
Like you reap any harvest from these labours
Unless you live as long as a patriarch?
    Why burden your existence
With cares for a future which you can't enjoy?
    In the time that's still permitted
Meditate on the errors you've committed,
Give up the long-term hope, the grandiose plan;
    What's hidden in the distance
Is *our* concern.' 'You couldn't be more wrong,'
Replied the eighty-year-old. 'The works of man
Are slow to grow and never last for long.
With bloodless hands the chill Fates play
The same game with your lives as with mine.
We're all alike allotted a brief stay.
Under the blue vault with its bright sunshine

Who can for certain say
That this is not his final day?
Is there one moment that can guarantee
The next? Enjoying their ease,
My grand-nephews will thank me for these trees.
Good Lord! Would you prevent a man of sense
From taking pains to please posterity?
That very thought's a fruit that I can chew
Today, perhaps tomorrow too,
Even – who knows? – for many days ahead.
Indeed, it may be I shall see the light
Of more than one dawn after you're all dead.'
  The old man proved right.
  Soon one of the three was drowned
Just out of port, America-bound;
  The second, trying to climb
In the service of the Army and the Crown
  To high office, was cut down
  By a bullet in his prime;
  And the third
Fell from a tree he was grafting to his doom.
The old man wept, and on their marble tomb
  Engraved the story you've just heard.

FABLE X

THE CRAYFISH AND HER DAUGHTER

Wise men sometimes make progress in the manner
Of crayfish, that is to say they turn their backs
On their objective. So the sailor tacks
To come to harbour, so the master planner,
To save his grand endeavour from detection,
Averts his face from where he's aiming for
And makes his enemy run in the wrong direction.
My metaphor's small, yet it applies to giants
In history – witness one conqueror
Who can frustrate unaided an alliance
Of a hundred heads, concealing what is not
His purpose and what is, until his plot
Ripens in victory. In vain the spies
To penetrate his secrets strain their eyes –
His movements are decrees of Fate, no more
Opposable than a great tidal bore.
A hundred lesser deities are unable
To match one Jove. King Louis seems to be

Just such a force – in tune with Destiny
He rules the universe. Now to my fable.

A crayfish remarked to her daughter one day:
'My goodness! Look at you! Can't you walk straight?'
    'Just look at yourself!' she replied.
    'I follow the family gait –
    Could I walk any other way?
Am I to march straight when you veer to one side?'

She was right. Heredity, of all the rules
That govern our lives, is the strongest; it applies
For good or ill in every mortal matter;
    It accounts for men being wise
    And men being fools,
    More commonly the latter.
To revert to turning one's back on one's objective –
    It can, especially in the case
    Of war, be extremely effective;
    But be sure you never face
The wrong way, at the wrong time or place!

FABLE XVI

THE FOREST AND THE WOODCUTTER

A woodcutter had split or else mislaid
    The haft of his axe's blade:
A loss which could have been in time repaired –
Time during which at least some trees
    Would have been spared.
At last he humbly asked the forest: 'Please,
As a favour, let me gently take
    Just one branch, to make
A new handle for my axe.' He would,
    He promised, chop his livelihood
Elsewhere in future and leave any pine or oak
Standing whose age and beauty were admired.
The innocent forest gave what he required.
She had cause to regret it; for the vandal,
    Armed with his fresh handle,
Used it to strip her of her sylvan pride.
    At each axe-stroke
The wood-nymph, tortured by her own gift, cried.

    That's the way of the world, the way
    Of worldly people. That's how they repay

Those who have done them good.
I'm tired of harping on it. But who wouldn't exclaim
    Against a sweet, shade-giving wood
    Being made the victim of such a crime?
        Alas, for a long time
        I have made myself hoarse,
        Even incurred some blame,
        By saying so. Ingratitude, brute force,
        Remain in fashion just the same.

FABLE XVII

THE FOX, THE WOLF AND THE HORSE

A fox, a young one but full of guile,
Seeing a horse for the first time,
Shouted to a wolf who was downright raw:
    'Come quickly, there's a gigantic, a sublime
    Animal grazing in our fields! My eyes
    Are still dazzled by what they saw.'
'Is it stronger than us?' asked the wolf with a knowing smile.
    'Describe it please. Be specific.'
    'If I were a painter or someone scientific,'
    The fox replied, 'I would try to adumbrate
    The pleasure and surprise
In store for you. But come. Who knows, it may have been sent
    As food for us by Fate.'
    Accordingly off they went.
Out to grass and about to kick up his heels and go,
At the sight of the pair the horse remained aloof.
'My lord,' said the fox, 'your humble servants would be glad to know
      Your name.'
    The other, not easily fooled,
Answered: 'Gentlemen, you are free to read it, for the same

Is inscribed by the smith on my sole.'
The fox at once apologized for his lack of knowledge.
'My parents,' he explained, 'never had me schooled.
They were poor; all they owned was a hole.
But the wolf's people are rich – he learnt reading at college.'

      Flattered by this speech,
      The wolf approached within reach.
His conceit cost him four teeth when a hoof
Unleashed a kick, and the horse vanished from view.
      There lay our wolf in the dirt,
      Bleeding and badly hurt.
      'Brother,' said the fox, 'here is proof
Of what thinking people have assured me is true.
That beast has just stamped on your jaw-bone:
      "The wise distrust the unknown".'

FABLE XVIII

THE FOX AND THE TURKEY-COCKS

A tree was serving roosting turkey-cocks
As a citadel against a raiding fox.
Circling the ramparts on his nightly prowl
And seeing on every perch a sentinel fowl,
The villain swore: 'Do they take me for a fool?
Shall they alone be exempt from Nature's rule?
No, by the gods, no!' His forecast proved right.
    The moon, being full and bright,
    Seemed to be taking the part
Of the turkeys against the fox that night.
No novice, though, in the besieger's art,
    Reynard, in this fix,
Dug deep into his bag of wicked tricks.
First he reared on his paws as if for a great leap,
Then he pretended to be dead or asleep,
    Then he sprang up, resurrected,
And cocked and waved his brush so it glittered in the ligh
And a dozen other bits of pantomime.
    Even Harlequin never affected
So many different roles in one night!
     In the meantime,

FABLE XIX

THE MONKEY

A monkey newly-wed in Paris,
Aping many a beast who marries,
Beat his poor wife. She sighed and cried
And then long-sufferingly died.
Their little boy began to bawl –
A useless, grotesque caterwaul.
The father laughed: his wife was dead
And he already had instead
Plenty of other girl-friends whom
He battered daily, I assume.
He haunted bars, became a soak.

Don't look for any good from folk
Who imitate, no matter what.
An author's worst of all the lot.

FABLE XX

THE SCYTHIAN PHILOSOPHER

A Scythian philosopher, a man
Of great austerity, conceived a plan
To make his way of life rather more pleasant.
He went to Greece, and there in his wanderings
Met an old man like Virgil's happy peasant –
So utterly serene and satisfied
That he evoked comparison with kings,
With the gods almost. The sage's pride and joy
Was a beautiful orchard-garden. On his land
His visitor found him, pruning-hook in hand,
Lopping this branch of a fruit-tree, trimming that,
Everywhere thinning Nature's surplus fat,
Sure in the knowledge that for all his trouble
She would in time repay him more than double.
    'But why this massacre?'
    Demanded the philosopher.
'What sense does it make? What good
Can it do to cripple the poor wood?
    I beg you, lay aside
    That instrument of shame

And let Time's sickle bring about the same
Result: those branches will be driftwood soon
    On Lethe's sombre tide.'
'Ah,' said the other, 'but I only prune
    What isn't needed:
The cut branch helps the tree I leave to stand.'
Back in his dreary native land,
The Scythian seized a bill-hook and proceeded
    To chop and slash for days on end
    And strongly recommend
    To all his friends and neighbours
Similar drastic, amputative labours.
    So he continued to prune
    The finest boughs in his orchard
    Regardless of reason, time or tide,
    New or old moon,
    Until the last tortured
    Tree withered and died.

My Scythian is a perfect exemplar
Of the Stoic follower who goes too far,
Who, for the passionate soul's own 'good,'
Hacks alike at its sound and rotten wood,
Down to its most innocent desires.
    For my part,
I raise my voice against these life-deniers
    Who with their knives
Sever the vital stalk that buoys the heart
And kill us long before our death arrives.

FABLE XXI

THE ELEPHANT AND JUPITER'S MONKEY

The elephant and the rhinoceros, having collided
        In a difference of opinion
Over their respective precedence and the boundaries of their dominion,
        Decided
To settle their quarrel by combat, hand-to-hand.
The great day came round, as planned,
When someone dashed up to announce
That Jupiter's winged monkey, wand in hand,
        Was about to land –
A simian named Gille, by all accounts.
At once the elephant, assuming he'd been sent
In the role of ambassador to investigate
The grandeur of the elephantine state
        And basking in the glow
Of this glorious thought, waited for the envoy to present
His credentials, and found him somewhat slow
        In appearing.
At last Mr Gille called by, casually, to salute
His Elephantship, who was all ready to grant a gracious hearing.
        The monkey, however, remained mute:
        Not a word about the dispute,

            No mention
Of the great topic which the king thought claimed the gods' attention
            (Elephant or fly –
            To them, what does the difference signify?)
            Seeing that he had no choice
            But to be the first to use his voice,
The elephant began: 'Soon my cousin Jupiter will enjoy the sight
            Of a tremendous fight
            From his supreme throne; all his court
            Will witness the fine sport.'
'What fight?' asked the monkey with a solemn face.
            'Good gracious, haven't you learned
The news? The rhino has challenged my pride of place,
And the tusked people are at war with the one-horned race.
Surely you've heard of our country – it's not without fame.'
'I should be enchanted to be informed of its name,'
            Mr Gille returned.
            'In our vast celestial hall
Matters like these are hardly discussed at all.'
The elephant, lost in amazement and shame,
Said: 'What are you doing, then, in the land of the elephants?'
'I've come to apportion a blade of grass among some ants.
There is nothing on which the gods don't lavish care:
Large and small are equal in their eyes.
            As for your affair,
It still hasn't been mooted in the skies.'

FABLE XXII

A FOOL AND A WISE MAN

A wise man, walking alone,
Was being bothered by a fool throwing stones at his head.
Turning to face him, he said:
'My dear chap, well thrown!
Please accept these few francs.
You've worked hard enough to get more than mere thanks.
Every effort deserves its reward.
But see that man over there? He can afford
More than I can.
Present him with some of your stones: they'll earn a good wage.'
Lured by the bait, the stupid man
Ran off to repeat the outrage
On the other worthy citizen.
This time he wasn't paid in money for his stones.
Up rushed serving-men,
And seized him and thrashed him and broke all his bones.

In the courts of kings there are pests like this, devoid of sense:
They'll make their master laugh at your expense.
To silence their cackle, should you hand out rough
Punishment? Maybe you're not strong enough.
Better persuade them to attack
Somebody else, who can more than pay them back.

MORE ABOUT PENGUINS
AND PELICANS

For further information about books available from Penguins please write to Dept EP, Penguin Books Ltd, Harmondsworth, Middlesex UB7 0DA.

In the U.S.A.: For a complete list of books available from Penguins in the United States write to Dept CS, Penguin Books, 625 Madison Avenue, New York, New York 10022.

In Canada: For a complete list of books available from Penguins in Canada write to Penguin Books Canada Ltd, 2801 John Street, Markham, Ontario L3R 1B4.

In Australia: For a complete list of books available from Penguins in Australia write to the Marketing Department, Penguin Books Australia Ltd, P.O. Box 257, Ringwood, Victoria 3134.

In New Zealand: For a complete list of books available from Penguins in New Zealand write to the Marketing Department, Penguin Books (N.Z.) Ltd, P.O. Box 4019, Auckland 10.